ROTTEN TO THE CORE

GHOST

Lock Down Publications and Ca$h Presents

ROTTEN TO THE CORE

A Novel by **GHOST**

Rotten To The Core

Lock Down Publications
P.O. Box 870494
Mesquite, Tx 75187

Visit our website
www.lockdownpublications.com

Lock Down Publications
Like our page on Facebook: Lock Down
Publications @

www.facebook.com/lockdownpublications.ldp

Cover design and layout by: **Dynasty Cover Me**
Book interior design by: **Shawn Walker**
Edited by: **LaSonya Smith**

Ghost

Stay Connected with Us!

Text **LOCKDOWN** to 22828 to stay up-to-date
with new releases, sneak peeks, contests and more...

Submission Guidelines:

Submit the first three chapters of your completed manuscript to ldpsubmissions@gmail.com, subject line: Your book's title. The manuscript must be in a .doc file and sent as an attachment. The document should be in Times New Roman, double-spaced and in size 12 font. Also, provide your synopsis and full contact information. If sending multiple submissions, they must each be in a separate email.

Have a story but no way to send it electronically? You can still submit to LDP/Ca$h Presents. Send in the first three chapters, written or typed, of your completed manuscript to:

LDP: Submissions Dept
Po Box 870494
Mesquite, Tx 75187

DO NOT send original manuscript. Must be a duplicate.

Provide your synopsis and a cover letter containing your full contact information.

Thanks for considering LDP and Ca$h Presents.

DEDICATION

This book is dedicated to my precious, beautiful
Babygirl. The love of my life, 3/10. Everything I do
is for YOU, first and foremost.

ACKNOWLEDGEMENTS

I would like to thank the Boss Man and C.E.O of LDP, Cash. Thank you for this opportunity. Your wisdom, motivation and encouragement are appreciated. Thanks, Bruh.

To the Queen and C.O.O of LDP, thank you for all that you do Sis. Your hard work, dedication and loyalty to this company never goes unnoticed.

Chapter 1

Jayden

Nico cocked his Forty Glock, placed the pistol back in his waistband, then wiggled his fingers into the black leather gloves that only an hour prior we'd stolen from Wilson's Leather Boutique. He adjusted the seat so that it was able to move backward a few inches, then took the seatbelt and pulled it across his body. The rain fell onto the roof of the stolen Buick Park Avenue that I'd hot-wired an hour earlier.

I felt the Forty-Five weighing heavy in the small of my back as I adjusted myself in the seat and took two more hits of the Syracuse Kush that we were blowing before handing it over to him. "Here you go, kid. I can see you all up tight and shit. You need to ease up. Word is bond." I laughed a little before frowning.

Lightning flashed across the Philadelphia sky, illuminating the dark alley that we were parked in. As the wind picked up, it caused the car to sway from right to left. A light whistling of air along with the pitter patter of rain drops that assaulted the roof and windshield of the car resonated to drown out the silence in between us.

Nico took the Dutch and pulled from it. "I'm good, Dun. Yo, I'm just ready to get this shit over with. That's it, that's all." He blew Kush smoke through his nostrils and inhaled it back into his mouth before blowing it out of his nose again.

Nico was six feet even, light skinned, mixed with Puerto Rican and Black. He had short but real

9

curly hair that he wore cut into a stylish, tapered Mohawk. Though at first glance he was thought to be a pretty boy, he was one of the deadliest dudes that I'd ever met in Philly, and he was only twenty-one years old. He was my right-hand man, and we'd been tight ever since we were six years old.

"Yo, you sure you ain't feeling some type of way because we gotta body this nigga? I mean, he is your sister Whitney's fiancé and all." I took the Dutch back when he handed it to me. I was already feeling higher than usual, and I figured it was because I hadn't eaten all this day, and by the time we were preparing to hit this lick, it was already eleven at night.

The rain picked up and got so bad that I could barely see out of the windows. It sounded like bags of rice were being poured on top of the stolen whip. I started to imagine myself drenched and got irritated, and then my stomach growled.

Nico sucked his teeth. "Fuck this nigga, kid. Word is bond. Son got them birds, and we need to get our paws on them. Whitney ain't ever gotta find out what went down with this clown. Besides, I don't like her working in his father's strip club anyway. I feel like this nigga recruited my sister, so we gotta get these chickens and get right. That way she won't have to work in that punk ass club just to make ends meet." He frowned and shook his head. "Yo, I'm tired of being a scrub, Jayden. It's too many niggas out in Philly eating and we ain't one of 'em. It's time to turn over a new leaf." He sniffed loudly and pulled on his nose with his thumb and forefinger. In addition to blowing Kush, the homey had a thing for tooting

OxyContin pills, and Percocet. He'd been shot more than ten times already and had gotten addicted to the opioids during one of his hospital stays.

I'd only been shot twice in the back, but I'd yet to grow addicted to any pain meds. That didn't come until later in life. "Yo, well, fuck this nigga then. Just in case you are feeling some type of way and wanna keep that to yourself, I ain't got no problem with sending him to the Reaper. You can keep yo' gun in yo' waistband. I'm getting that heroin up out of him by any means. You already know how I get down." I nodded and felt my heart already pounding in my chest like an 808 bass drum. I was ready to get the show on the road. Ready to get away with them birds that I knew Lincoln kept stashed in his Band-o. It was time to eat, and I wasn't pushing away from the table until I burped.

"Yeah, I already know, lil' bruh. That's the reason I picked you to ride out with me. I was gon' handle this nigga on my own, but I figure, why not rip this nigga into shreds with my right-hand man, nah' mean?" He smiled, then zipped up his Gucci jacket. "Come on, it's time."

I took three hard pulls from the Dutch then stubbed it out in the ashtray. Afterward, I released my seat belt and zipped up my Marc Jacobs light spring jacket before pushing open the driver's door; rushing out into the rain, jogging behind Nico as it felt like I was being sprayed by a fireman's hose.

By the time we got to the back of Lincoln's house, I was drenched and freezing. The wind seemed to pick up speed again. I had to turn my back to it as Nico beat on the back door with eight loud pounds.

"Yo, remember, you don't do nothing without me winking at you. After I wink, all bets are off. Handle yo' business and I'll handle mine." He turned his back to the wind and pounded on the door again.

About a minute later, it cracked open. "Who is it?" A deep voice asked from behind the wooden door.

Nico pulled his hood back a little. "Yo, it's Nico, tell Lincoln that I'm here and to hurry up cuz it's pouring down out here like a muhfucka."

The door slammed back as I pulled my hood further down to cover my head and a bit of my face. The thunder roared in the clouds as lightning flashed across the sky. "Yo, just for this nigga making us wait outside in this storm like this, I'm putting a few in his face. Word is bond. You know I hate the cold." I said shivering and blowing into my gloves. I felt my temper getting hotter by the second. I hated when niggas who were a lil' deeper into the game than me tried to treat me like a bitch, and that's exactly what I felt me, and Nico were being treated as. I didn't like that shit.

The back door opened, and Lincoln stood with a big smile on his dark-skinned face. He reminded me of a taller version of Kendrick Lamar. "Yo, what's good, Nico?" He stood to the side. "Y'all come on in and get out of that storm."

Nico stepped into the hallway first, and then me right behind him.

I watched them hug, then me and Lincoln shook up and I gave him a hug too. "What's good, nigga? Long time no see." I said, disliking the embrace. I didn't like all that affectionate shit from one man to another. I felt that the bump of a fist was enough. All that hugging shit was over the top in my opinion but seeing as we were about to rip this nigga off, I had to do what I had to.

Lincoln laughed and closed the door behind us, placing a big two by four across it. "I'm surprised my brother got you to roll with him. You're a real solo-dolo type of dude. But it's good." He waved us to follow him as he ascended the steps and into the house.

There was an older man with a bottle of Korbel in his hand, getting ready to bring it to his lips. I could tell right away that he was of some kin to Lincoln because they resembled each other.

"Yo, this my pops right here. He down from New York. Y'all say what's good. Pops. this Nico, Whitney's brother, and this his right-hand man, Jayden. They thick as thieves and basically our family now."

Nico grabbed his hand and gave him a half hug while I bumped fists with him and kept it moving.

We wound up in the basement, sitting on a couch while music videos played across the sixty-inch smart screen television that Lincoln had in his basement. He also had a red lightbulb screwed into the light socket.

He handed me a blunt that was stuffed with the Syracuse weed that we'd been smoking earlier. "I just copped fifty pounds of this shit. I should have it by the end of the week. When I get it, I'ma throw a few pounds your way, Nico. I know you trying to handle yo' business on that green tip too, so I'ma get you right." He smiled and handed Nico a stuffed blunt.

Nico nodded and rubbed his chin. "That sound good, but you already know why I'm here. I'm trying to cop a few birds and buss some moves. What's good? You told me to come and holler at you and you was gon' put me down." He took his lighter and lit the tip of the blunt before inhaling it deeply.

Lincoln laughed. "Yo, take it easy, kid. I know what you came through for. I mean, I ain't know you was gon' bring no company, but it is what it is." He sat on another couch directly across from where me and Nico were sitting. I took offense to his comment about me being company right away. I felt my blood boiling and I was trying hard to be easy.

Nico shook his head. "First of all, this my nigga. He ain't no company. Secondly, never tell me to take it easy, or call me kid in the way you just did. Holler at me at eye level, Lincoln. That's the only way all this shit gon' work between us."

Lincoln's father came down the steps and into the basement as Nico was saying the last part. I noted right away that he had a shoulder holster on that held two pistols. Both holsters were filled with .9-millimeter hand guns. Just seeing that made me feel like he was trying to intimidate me and the homey. Now my vision was going hazy because I was getting more and more angry. I already didn't like other niggas, but for a muhfucka to think they could expose that they were armed and that it would make me and the homey fearful or some shit had me ready to blow. I didn't know how much longer I could sit there without erupting like a volcano.

"Son, you okay down here?" He asked standing behind us, mugging me and Nico. I almost found him hilarious because he ain't have the slightest idea of what was going on in my head.

Lincoln looked over his shoulder at his father, down to his guns, and back to us with a smile on his face. "I'm good, pops. These niggas just playing. They don't know that goon shit run in our family like it do, nah' mean?" He said looking Nico in the eyes.

Nico nodded, looked over to me and laughed. "You hear this nigga? That shit sound like a threat to you, bruh?" He winked three times, and it was all I needed to gain some relief from my anger.

I jumped up from the couch before anybody could react, cocked the hammer on my Forty-Five, aimed it at his father and pulled the trigger twice. *Boom. Boom.* It knocked a chunk of meat out of his old man's shoulder, causing his to turn in a one eighty, before I jumped over the table and was staring down at him with my gun smoking. "Tough ass nigga, don't move." I leaned down and took the .9-millimeter out of his holster while he winced on the ground in pain.

He turned on to his side and tried to look up at me but was caught by the bottom of my Timberland boot as I stepped on his face and forced it to the ground.

Nico had his pistol aimed at Lincoln, and Lincoln had his hands in the air, shaking like a leaf. "Nigga, I told you before you even started fucking with my sister that all of that tough shit was gon' get you in trouble one day. Don't you know that you fucking with pure goons?" He asked standing up and pushing the table to the side, so he could walk across to Lincoln. He extended his arm and pressed the barrel of his gun to Lincoln's cheek. "Where the fuck them chickens at?"

Lincoln's father began to groan louder as more blood poured out of his shoulder. "Uhh, uhh. I thought you said they were family. Uhh. What the fuck kind of family get down like this?" He groaned.

Lincoln looked up at Nico with a mug on his face. "So, this how you get down, nigga? You that thirsty to get into the game that you gotta pull some shit like this?" He questioned, curling his lip.

Nico grabbed a handful of his air and spat in his face. "Bitch nigga, fuck you. Where them chickens at?" He yanked him to his feet by his hair.

Lincoln swallowed and bit into his bottom lip. "Nah, nigga, you see, I know better. I know if I give you what you want, you ain't gon' do shit but kill me anyway. The streets talk. I know how you get down. I just thought that since we were family and all that I could give you the benefit of the doubt, but silly me, huh?" He sucked his teeth loudly.

"Yo, Nico, this nigga doing plenty of talking, kid. Either make that nigga give us what we came for, or I will. Word is bond, time is money." I said getting vexed.

Nico took his pistol and slapped it across Lincoln's face so hard that it put a large gash in it. "Take me to them birds right now, or I'm popping you!" He hollered.

Lincoln fell to his knees and stayed there while Nico tried to pull him back up. "Fuck you, nigga. Kill me. I'll be damned if I give you my stash and you kill

16

me anyway." He spat blood across the concrete and wiped his mouth.

Nico slung him to the floor, straddled him, and began to pistol-whip him with the handle of his gun, repeatedly. I watched blood pop into the air and all along Nico's neck, but it didn't make him stop. I saw that his eyes were blank. He was in a zone with his teeth bared.

Lincoln's father turned onto his back. "Stop, stop, stop. Please, don't kill my baby, man. I'll take you to the merch. It's upstairs in the mattress. Lord, please, don't let them kill my baby." The man whimpered, and I prayed that if I ever met the fate that they were, that my old man would never bitch up the way that he was. A man should never hear his father sound worse than a woman in distress. It was sickening to me.

I yanked him up by the shirt and threw him into the wall, taking the barrel of my gun and forcing it into his gunshot wound, listening to him holler at the top of his lungs. "You finna take me upstairs to this stash, and if it's there then you'll leave this situation with your life. You got that, pops?" I flung him toward the stairs before looking over my shoulder to see Nico beating Lincoln to death. Lincoln's face was already caved in, and I doubted that he was alive by that point. I simply shrugged and forced his father up the steps.

We made it to the second-floor landing before he opened the door to Lincoln's bedroom, and fell onto the carpet, dizzy from blood loss. "It's in the mattress. Just flip it, then get me and my son to a hospital." He said, with his eyes rolling into the back of his head.

I placed my bloody gun into the small of my back, took the mattress and flipped it onto him before searching all around it for a seam that could have been opened for easy storing. After taking a few minutes and not finding one, I grew irritated. "Ahhh! Where the fuck is it?" I hollered, moving the mattress so I could look down at him.

He was so weak that all he could do was point to the box spring. I looked behind me, kneeled, and flipped it over. As soon as I did, two silver packages fell onto the carpet. My eyes grew wider, and the beats of my heart sped up. I couldn't believe it. I turned the box spring all the way over and saw the poor duct tape job that Lincoln had done to conceal his product. I got to ripping the tape away, causing one brick after the next to fallout of it. There were six in total. Once I couldn't locate any more, I took those six and wrapped them in the sheet from the bed, tying it in a knot before standing back up and looking down at his father.

The man was on his back, struggling to breathe. He had a puddle of blood around him and more oozing out of his shoulder at a rapid pace. He coughed and sat halfway up before falling backward. "Call. The. Ambulance." He whispered.

I frowned. "Where the money at, old man?" I asked, kicking the bottom of his shoe. "You hear me?"

He coughed once again, and a thick glob of blood slowly poured out of his gaping mouth. Then, he was choking, holding his neck. His chest heaved, his eyes were bucked, and he kept inhaling loudly.

I ain't have time for all of that. I didn't feel like he could help me any further, so I tore up the room, digging my hand into the mattress and box spring, only coming up with about ten bands. I threw it into my pocket before standing over him as he lay still with is eyes wide open. I didn't know if he was dead or not, but I couldn't take any chances, so I kneeled after taking the pillow from the bed, placed it over his face and fired my gun twice, watching his body jerk before I ran out of the room and back into the basement.

Nico was just getting up from straddling Lincoln's dead body. He'd beaten him into a bloody pulp. I looked down and saw that Lincoln was now unrecognizable.

"Bruh, I got everything. Let's get the fuck out of here!" I hollered over to him, ready to get as far away from that house as possible.

Nico looked as if he was in a trance. He shook his head real hard, then looked over to me. "Yo, what you say?" He wiped Lincoln's blood from his lips with the back of his gloved hand. His pistol was the color of red as if it had been dipped into some burgundy paint.

"I said I got everything. Let's go!" I ran up the stairs, looking over my shoulder to see him still frozen in place. "Nico! Let's go, nigga!" I hollered, growing impatient.

He finally snapped out of it and ran behind me, with us both hurrying into the rain where we ran full speed down the alley, while thunder roared in the

Ghost

sky, and the rain felt as if it was transitioning into hail.

Chapter 2

I felt like I was getting ready to throw up. We hadn't been back inside the Buick for more than five minutes before there were a pair of red and blue lights flashing behind us. I stepped on the gas and turned a corner so hard that the car almost rolled over. It fishtailed before straightening, and then I was stepping on the gas again.

"Fuck, fuck, fuck!" Nico hollered. "What you think they getting at us for? Because of the stolen whip, or the move we just bussed?" He asked sounding as if he was ready to freak all the way out. He looked over his shoulder and shook his head.

Errr-h! I slammed on the brakes as I neared an intersection that was busy with cars. Our car slid nearly into traffic before coming to a halt. "I don't know, bruh, but we can't go down like this. Nigga, it's two bodies back there. That's two life sentences for the both of us." I said, throwing the car into reverse, just enough to back up so I could hit a right and drive alongside the side walk until I was able to merge onto the busy intersection. The police attempted the same move behind us as my windshield wipers suddenly died. "Fuck!"

Nico shook his head, looking behind us. "It's three of them back there now, Jayden. Man, this shit don't look good. We gotta come from under this. I'm finna start bussing." He said rolling down his window, drawing his from his waistband.

I could barely see out of the windshield. I felt that in any moment I was getting ready to crash. "Nigga, if you start shooting then they gon' get to

shooting, and they got way more bullets than we do."
I said, turning the corner and side-swiping a Yukon
Denali truck. I stepped on the gas and hit a left into
an alley, flooring the pedal. The car jerked and shot
forward.

Nico kept on looking backward and shaking his
head. "They in the alley now, bruh. Look, ain't no
reason both of us should go down for this shit. I'ma
take the heat, and you just take this merch and get me
a good lawyer. Can I count on you to do that?" He
asked looking over his shoulder again.

I shot out of one alley and into another one. The
car jumped in the air and came back down violently
with sparks coming from under it as I stepped on the
gas again. "Bruh, what you talking about? We in this
shit together." I said, struggling to see. The car
slammed into a garbage can that was in the middle of
the alley, sending it into the sky. I swerved a little
and nearly lost the handle of the wheel but regained
it just in time.

Nico shook his head. "Listen to me, Jayden. I
need you to make sure that my mother and my sister
are good until I get back out. My mother struggling
with them bills, and I hate seeing that shit, man.
Then, Whitney lost; need a lot of direction. Keep her
away from them fuck niggas." He spat.

I sped out of the alley, hitting a hard right on
the side street, before stepping on the gas again. The
tires spun for a brief second before the car lurched
forward, regaining its traction. I stormed down the
street as the police cars continued to follow in hot
pursuit. I was on the verge of panicking. As I drove
down the side street, two more police cars were

coming in our direction. I feared that one of them would slam into us, so I slammed on the brakes, causing the car to skid before I made a left and wound back up in another one of Philly's alleys.

Looking in my rear-view mirror I saw that the police did the same thing. "Look, Nico, you got more people to support than I do. All I got is my mother, so jump out and I'll take the fall." I said, not entirely sure if I wanted to do that or not. The last thing I wanted was to be sitting in one of Pennsylvania's prisons for the rest of my life, but it was all I could say to save face.

I stormed down the alley and came to its end, paused for a second and drove into the next one, not knowing where the hell I was going.

Nico looked over his shoulder again as I made a crazy left and cut through an open field that had once been a house. The wet grass sounded slushy under the tires. After I came from out of it I was back onto the side street and flooring the gas. Looking into my rear-view mirror, I couldn't see a berry in sight.

"Nah, bruh, trust me on this one. I'm gon' come from under this shit. I got my reasons. Make a left up there and jump out. Hear, take this shit with you." He said, reaching into the backseat and setting the sheet filled with heroin on his lap.

I sped down the street and made a left just as he asked me to, storming down that block before slowing down. "You crazy, bruh. I don't know what you up to, but I got you. Don't worry about shit, that's my word." I said stopping the car, and throwing it in park, then grabbing the sheet of dope off his lap and opening my driver's door.

"Jayden! Listen, man, stack them chips and get me a good lawyer if I get caught up. Take care of my people, and don't fuck my sister, dawg. That's a cardinal rule. We're brothers, nigga, so that'll be like incest, and we're better than that. You got me?" He asked looking me in the eyes as the sirens blared somewhere off in the distance.

I grabbed his hand and pulled him into a side hug, kissing him on the cheek. "I got you, bruh. Man, I love you too, nigga. I won't fail you." I hugged him again, then broke the embrace, opening my driver's side door wide preparing to get out.

He nodded. "I love you too, kid. Don't let me rot in that muhfucka if I get pinched, even though I don't plan on that happening." He curled his upper lip and looked behind us.

"Yo, I got you. Your family is my family until you touch down. I'll make sure you're good, too. Love, nigga." I jumped out of the car and crouched down as he peeled away from the curb and flew down the street.

I stayed alongside the parked cars as the lightning flashed across the sky and thunder roared behind the clouds. Finding a Suburban truck, I slid under it and laid on my back, just as two police cars sped past, giving chase to Nico. I stayed there for about ten minutes, waited until the coast was clear, then jumped up and made my way through one alley at a time in the storm, until I made it home an hour later.

I was soaked and felt like I was going to be sick. My chest hurt, and my stomach felt as if I was coming down with the stomach flu, but all that mattered was that I was home, safe and sound.

* * *

Three days later, and after Nico had been apprehended by Philly's finest, I found myself standing behind his mother as she sat on the metal stool, waiting for him to come to the other side of the glass so she could speak to him. I'd been by her side from the time he'd called her from the county jail, stating that he'd been booked in on charges of fleeing and alluding law enforcement, possession of a firearm by a felon, and reckless endangerment because of the high-speed chase. Nico had been the family's bread winner, so I was sure that his mother was on the verge of panicking.

I saw the correctional officer guiding him by the arm, then sitting him before her. He looked real rough. His curls looked dry, and they were all over the place. He also looked as if he'd lost a few pounds.

Janet grabbed the phone right away and put it to her ear. "Nico. Nico, baby, talk to me." She cried, and it made me feel horrible.

Nico grabbed the phone and placed it to his ear. I saw his lips moving but I couldn't tell what he was saying. I was so nervous to be inside the courthouse that I was sweating bullets. I felt that in any second, they would grab ahold of me and place me within one of the cells right next to his, and I wasn't going for that shit. I would make them kill me first.

Janet exhaled. "How can they do that, baby? I thought you were innocent until proven guilty. That's not fair." She cried, lowering her head as tears sailed down her cheeks.

Nico's lips were moving again. I looked from him and surveyed the visiting area, just as a thick ass caramel sista came into the door with some Fendi jeans so tight that I couldn't take my eyes away from her. We made eye contact before she looked me up and down and licked her juicy lips, smiling, looking fine as hell. I waited until she walked past me and looked down at that fat ass booty. The muhfucka was round and perked up nicely, before it led downward into a thick pair of thighs. I shook my head and exhaled loudly as she found one of the booths and sat in front of a phone.

"Jayden, here. Nico wanna talk to you." Janet said standing up and handing me the phone. She dabbed at the corners of her eyes with a tissue. Sniveling and shaking her head, she told me, "I'm finna lose my baby to the system. Why me, Lord? Why my child?" she asked, looking at the ceiling.

I sat down and placed the phone to my ear. "What's good, bruh?"

Nico shook his head and held his forehead. "It's all bad, Jayden, and I don't think my moms finna be able to handle this shit. They already telling me that my PO putting a hold on me, and ain't about to lift it. She's going for revocation based off the charges I'm facing alone." He shook his head. "Fuck."

I swallowed and remained silent. I didn't really know what to say to the homey. I mean, he'd volunteered to ride off in that car on his own. Now he was on the inside and I was out. "Bruh, why you ain't get rid of the heat? What made you hold on to that burner?" I asked barely above a whisper. I was trying to make sure that Janet didn't hear me, but I was sure that she couldn't because she was too busy in tears, sobbing loudly.

He lowered his head. "I was fucked up that night, bruh. Them pills had me fucked up. Had I been in my right mind, I would have tossed that bitch or told you to take it with you. Once they run it, I'm done. I got a few bodies on it." He shook his head. "Anyway, my bail hearing today but I already know whether they give me one or not, my PO gon' break that shit up. I'm cooked. Take my mother home and make sure she good. She don't need to see me go through this shit. Her rent is due in a week. It's twelve hundred, plus she got some more bills. Just do what you can until I can figure some shit out. I know I'm finna get hit hard, kid, but I got some shit up my sleeve. I'ma need a good lawyer that might run you fifty gees. Do whatever it takes to make that happen, and I'll handle my end of things in here. It's a few of Meek's people that say I can handle some business for 'em, and they can get me the help I need. I don't know what that mean, but I'm all ears. You heard anything about Lincoln 'nem?" He asked, mouthing Lincoln's name, and not saying it.

I nodded. "Yeah, they been snatched up already, but so far so good. If I was you, I wouldn't focus on that. We should be straight. I wish I would have known that the law was sweating us because of the stolen whip and not that. I would have pulled over and let me jump out of the whip with the merch." I lied, because I would have done none of the sort. I couldn't see myself sitting where he was. I just didn't have that shit in me.

He nodded. "Yeah, but it is what it is. How is Whitney doing?" He looked me over closely.

I shrugged. "Ever since Lincoln went down, she been planning his funeral. I think she'll be okay in time, but for right now, I can't really tell one way or the other."

He took a deep breath and exhaled. "Well, make sure she's straight too, and like I said, hit them bills for me and grab that lawyer. I'll handle this end. Loyalty, my nigga, and I love you, kid."

I nodded. "I love you too, bruh, and I'm on it. You already know that."

I handed Janet the phone, so she could say her goodbyes. I made eye contact with the thick ass caramel sista again, and she smiled. She ran her tongue across her lips again before looking back across at the nigga she was sitting in front of. I blew air through my teeth and walked over to where she was seated, just as she was telling whoever was on the other side of the glass that thirty years wasn't that long for her to wait. That she would just take it one day at a time until his appeal went through.

I stopped two steps away from her. "Yo, fuck that nigga. I'm here right now, so what's good?" I asked, looking down into her pretty face.

She even smelled good. Her scent was intoxicating.

Some heavy-set, dark skinned nigga started beating on the glass like he was mad or something.

I looked at him and mugged the fuck out of him before turning my gaze back upon her. "You heard me?"

She bucked her eyes and remained silent. Through the phone I could hear the fat nigga going nuts. He was hollering at the top of his lungs, slobbering all at the mouth.

I took the phone out of her hand and hung it up, then pulled her to her feet by her wrist. She ain't put up no resistance. "My name Jayden, and I'm gon' take over from where that nigga left off. What's your name?" I asked, kissing the back of her hand. I don't know where that came from because prior to that day I had never done anything like that. I think I was just mesmerized by how bad she was.

She took one look over her shoulder, back at the big gorilla, before sighing and walking into my direction. The curls on her head bouncing with each step. "My name is Jazz, and that was my high school sweetheart. He gon' be mad at me. I better go back." She said, looking over her shoulder at him.

The guards had come to restrain him. He started to fight them off, hollering, though I couldn't hear shit he was saying because he was on the other side of the glass.

I shook my head and pulled her further in my direction. "He can't do nothing for you now. You need to let me step in and find out what I'm about. I can tell you a high maintenance kind of female; about your paper, right?" I asked sizing her up and down.

By the look of her, I could tell, she would be the cause of any nigga falling off his square. She was that breathtakingly beautiful, with her small waist and nice hips. Her breasts molded themselves against her Fendi top. Both nipples were visible. I could have her set up a hunnit top notch hustlers, so I could tear they ass off. I had to get her into my stable. I would be able to make some serious dough in a short amount of time because most niggas thought with their dicks instead of their brains. Because of that, it wouldn't take long until I was seeing crazy numbers.

Jazz watched as they drug the big gorilla out of the visiting area, slamming the big metal doors behind them. "Look, I don't know you, but if you're talking about money, then you got my ear. I'm accustomed to getting it on my own the hard way, but if you got some shortcuts, then maybe we should have a coffee or something." She looked up at me with her pretty brown eyes and popped back on her legs just as Janet stood up from Nico's booth and walked over to me, placing her arm around my waist.

"Aight, well, let's go out here and exchange information, and we'll go from there, since we're talking the same language."

"Baby, let's get out of here. I'm getting more and more depressed just being in this building." Janet said, laying her head on my chest.

Jazz frowned. "Let's get right, homey, and I'll be in touch. That way you can go and make sure your mother's straight."

Before I left, we wound up exchanging numbers, and so started one of the most lucrative relationships that I had ever formed.

***

Later that day, Nico was denied bail, and within less than twenty-four hours his probation officer put in the papers to have him revoked. Three weeks after his bail denial, he was revoked and sent back to prison to serve the remaining year of probation, while he had the other charges looming over his head. As soon as I got the news, I felt sick as hell. It took me three days to eat a meal. I knew that I had to get out there and grind for the homey, so I could no longer sit back and lay low. I had to hit the streets of Philly like a savage to get my mans the things that he needed.

Chapter 3

In the fourth week, after Nico's bail denial, I felt like it was time for me to hit the slums and get my feet wet in the game. The police were still investigating Lincoln and his father's murder, but at this point they were still without any leads, and I was thankful for that. I kept my ear to the streets, and from as much as I could tell there wasn't anybody screaming me or Nico's name for the hit, so it was time to get money.

I spent two whole days bussing down a kilo of heroin and aluminum foiling up about twenty gees worth of product. After I finished, I placed all the merch within a big Ziploc bag and stuffed it in the bottom of the dresser drawer I had inside of the guest room where I stayed in at Janet's house. Because she was going through it so bad, emotionally, Nico thought it would be in her best interest for me to chill there for a few months, or at least until she was able to mentally grasp the concept that her only son and provider was gone for at least a year.

I think having me there made her feel closer to him. I don't know why, but I think that was just the case. The same night that I'd finished foiling up the heroin, I decided to take a shower, so I could turn in early because I was already considering on waking up at the crack of dawn and hitting up the avenue, right outside of Skid Row. In Philly, that's where a lot of the heroin addicts liked to post up, so I knew I could pick up some nice money before the sun was even all the way in the sky.

As I was coming out of the shower and walking back into the guest room with just a towel around my body, I was met by Janet who was sitting on the edge of the guest room's bed, with a short, silk, red night gown on that barely covered her thick thighs. Her legs were crossed and that brought the hem of the gown all the way upward and just below her crotch. The material was so sheer that I could clearly make out each of her big brown nipples. They appeared to be erect as they poked up against the gown's front. She had a glass of wine in one hand and a blunt in the other one.

I paused in the door way and looked her over closely, in a state of confusion. "Janet, what's good with you?" I asked walking into the room and opening my top drawer, so I could take out a pair of Polo boxers. I looked at her over my shoulder.

She licked her juicy lips and uncrossed her thick thighs, only to re-cross them again, flashing me and exposing the fact that she was without any panties. "I'm horny, Jayden, and I'm hoping you gon' do somethin' about that." She said, opening her legs and pulling the hem of her gown upward, placing her right foot on the bed.

I turned around and looked into her eyes first, before trailing them downward and drinking in the sight of her meaty pussy. The lips were puffy, covered with faint pubic hair that didn't do enough to hide their deep brown complexion.

She took her left hand, after putting the blunt in her mouth, and rubbed all over her sex. "Why don't you drop that towel and let me see what working with?" She reached and placed the blunt and the glass of wine on the night table, then looked over at me,

34

rubbing her thighs together. She sucked on her bottom lip and looked me right in the eyes.

I felt my dick swelling underneath my towel. I'd always thought that Nico's mother was fine as hell on all levels. She was thick, kept herself in shape, and on top of that, her face was as hell just like her daughter's. I often tried my best to not watch her when she walked around the house in next to nothing, which she did on a regular basis. Sometimes I wondered if she really knew how bad she was, or if she was oblivious to that fact.

I laughed nervously. "Janet, stop playing with me. You like my mother or something. I been knowing you ever since I was six years old. I can't look at you like that." I grabbed my boxers out and placed them on my shoulder, preparing to go into the bathroom so I could change into them, even though my dick kept throbbing underneath my towel.

I couldn't get the image of her sex lips out of my mind. They looked so good, that every part of me wanted to slide in between them suckers, but I had to keep in mind the respect that I had for Nico.

Janet bounced off the bed and slowly walked over to me, with her gown around her waist. I watched her sex lips smush into each other with each step that she took. Her thick thighs jiggled, her pretty toes sunk into the carpet, and one of the straps fell from her shoulder, exposing more of her brown breast.

She got into my face, looking me in the eyes. "Nico said that while he's gon' you're supposed to take care of me. He said that you would hold this house down just as he would." She reached and rubbed along the front of my towel until she was cuffing my dick into her little hand. At feeling the width of it, she moaned deep within her throat, then trailed her hand downward to see how long I was. That made her close her eyes, and once again she ran her long tongue across her lips. "Umm, you gotta give me some of this." She yanked the towel away and looked down with her eyes bucked.

I looked out at her and saw the way her nipples were poking up against the material of the gown, and how thick her thighs were, and the way her sex lips looked as if they were breathing and I couldn't take anymore. I had to have her thick ass, especially when she dropped down to her knees, stroking my dick, running the head all over her lips.

I grabbed a handful of her hair. "Open yo' mouth and put it in there, Janet. You gon' make me do this shit, you better suck the hell out of this dick." I demanded, sliding into her mouth, and stepping on to my tippy toes.

She licked all over the head, then pursed her lips and started to suck me at full speed, before popping me out of her mouth. "I will, baby. I'ma suck this dick just like I'm supposed to. Just watch me. Then, you gotta fuck me as hard as you can, because I ain't supposed to be doing this. Punish me." She popped me back into her mouth and got to moaning around my dick while she sucked me at full speed.

She was spearing her head into my lap, looking me in the eyes, then popping me out and stroking it while she kissed up and down it. Then, she was sucking on the head so hard that I was on the verge of coming already. I had to close my eyes because both of her shoulder straps had fallen, and her titties were out in the open, wobbling on her chest with both nipples erect. The areolas were huge. She looked so damn hot on her knees like that.

She popped me out again. "Tell me you love it, Jayden. Tell me you love how I'm putting it down on you, baby, because I love it." She moaned, then sucked me back into her mouth and got to going full speed while stroking it. She took her hand and ran it up and down my thighs, squeezing them, with her jaws hollowed out.

I grabbed her hair more aggressively and humped into her mouth faster and faster, feeling myself on the verge of releasing my seed. I couldn't believe that my right-hand man's mother was giving me brains, and some of the best I'd ever had up to that point. "Unn, unn, uh, damn, Janet, here it come. You betta pull back." I groaned breathlessly, not wanting to cum in her mouth out of respect for her. I tried to back up, but she kept a hold of my dick, and pulled me closer to her, sucking me like a porno star. My eyes rolled into the back of my head, and then I was coming in spurts. "Un, un, un, aww, damn."

She sucked me harder and pumped my pipe with a tight, closed fist, milking me for every drop of my seed, sending tingles all throughout my body. She moaned all around it, then slowly pulled it out of her mouth. Looking down at the head, she took her fist and starting from my base, moving it upward so that a drop of semen appeared on top. She took her tongue and licked it off. "Umm, that's that fresh shit right there. Damn, you taste so good, baby." She kissed the head, then looked up at me. "You ready to fuck me now?" She stroked my pipe up and down, getting it back hard. It had barely lost any of its length to begin with.

I wanted to be in her body. I wanted to fuck this vet to let her know that it wasn't sweet; that I got down just like she got down. I grabbed a handful of her hair and forced her to her feet. She yelped and kept her head bent backward. I leaned down and sucked on her neck before biting it. "You want me to be the man of this house, right?" I asked, pushing her on to the bed so that she landed on her stomach, looking over her shoulder at me. "Spread them muhfucking thighs and let me see that pussy from the back." I growled, walking behind her.

She slowly slid her thighs apart until her sex lips were exposed. I noted the juices already on them. A trail of it slid down her right thigh and wound up on the side of her knee.

"What you finna do to me Jayden?" She asked reaching under herself and playing with her pussy. She squeezed her sex lips, then opened them wide, exposing her bubble gum pink interior, before I watched her finger go around and around her erect clitoris.

I kneeled and placed my nose right on her pussy hole and inhaled her scent. She smelled like she was ready to be fucked. The juices from her center stuck to my cheek and ran down my chin. I took my hands and opened her ass wide, before licking up and down her crease while she moaned at the top of her lungs.

"Unn-a! Yes, baby. Do me. Do me, baby. I need you so bad. Unn-a, fuck yes!" She arched her back and spread her knees wider.

I sucked first one pussy lip, and then the other, running my tongue in and out of her hot hole, tasting her saltiness and loving it. Then I trailed my tongue upward and licked all around her asshole as well, smacking her on her chubby cheeks, watching them vibrate from my assaults.

"Unn-a, my clit, Jayden. Suck my clit. Please, baby. Mommy need that. I'm so close." She whimpered, opening her sex lips wider for me to do my thing.

I stuck my face all the way into her crotch, trapped her clit with my lips, and pulled on it as if it were a nipple. Her juices skeeted into my mouth, and that motivated me to go harder; nipping at it with my teeth, and that seemed to drive her crazy.

"Uhh, uhh, ooo-a shit. I'm cumming, baby. I'm cumming. Uhh-shit!" She screamed, arching her back.

I took two fingers and shoved them inside of her hot pussy and got to fucking them in and out of her at full speed, while my lips continued to suck on her clit as if I was trying to get some milk out of it. She pushed backward into my face and cursed me out while she came and came.

I stood up and got behind her, grabbed a handful of her hair once again, pulled on it so that her back arched, then took my dick and placed the head right on her hole. "Beg me for this dick, Janet. Tell me you want me to fuck the shit out of you. Hurry up before I change my mind." I said, running my head up and down her dripping crease. It felt like a silk furnace.

"Uhhh! Please fuck me, baby. I need you! Fuck me hard or get the fuck out of my house!" She screamed, biting on her bottom lip.

I saw the way her hard nipples rubbed against the bed sheet, and for some reason it drove me crazy. She tried to reach under herself to force me in, but it was too late. With one motion, I slammed forward and implanted my dick deep within her hot, velvety womb, causing her to yelp in a pleasure-like pain. I grabbed a handful of her hair in one hand, and her hips with the other. I pounded her pussy like the pavement. *Bam, bam, bam, bam.* Again, and again. Her walls sucked at me. Her ass cheeks slammed into my lap. They felt like hot ass pillows. Our combined scents wafted into the air, making the whole scene a reality for me.

I still could not believe that I was fucking a woman I had been lusting after ever since I was six years old. The fact that it was Nico's mother, only added flames to the fire that was burning deep within my bones.

I sped up the pace and took ahold of her hips with both of my hands, going as deep as I could while her juices dripped from my balls and down my legs.

"Yes, yes, yes, yes, fuck me, Jayden, yes, baby, fuck mommy. This shit yours. You the man. Of. This. House. Uhhh-a!" She screamed, bouncing back into me.

I slammed forward, watching my dick go in and out of her pussy. The lips opened and sucked me in. Every time I pulled back, her juices would pour out of her, then as I plunged forward they would attach themselves to my thighs and run down them. I smacked her ass once, then two times in a row. Afterward, I reached under her body to take a hold of her right titties, pulling on the nipple.

"Uhhh-a! I'm cumming, Jayden! I'm cumming! Uhhh-a fuck! I'm cumming!"

I slammed into her harder and harder while her pussy vibrated and sucked at me, and then I was coming hard.

"Yes, yes, yes, cum in me! Yes, baby, I love it! I love it. So. Fucking. Much." She moaned, humping back into me.

After our fucking session, she crawled into my bed and asked me to hold her, which I ain't have no problem doing. I felt a lil' guilty at first, you know, fucking my nigga's mama and all, but it was like she's said. Nico told her that I was gon' hold her down in every way. I didn't think he was expecting for me to be fucking her or nothin', but it was what it was. I enjoyed it. That vet pussy was good, and I intended on hitting it more than once. I'm just being honest.

Janet scooted her ass backward into my lap, then reached around herself and grabbed my arm, pulling it around her lower waist. "I knew you could fuck, Jayden, but I didn't think you was gon' put it down like that. I definitely needed it." She said, moving her ass up and down, causing my pipe to swell back up.

I reached upward and cuffed her left titty, feeling the weight of it. "You got some good pussy. I wasn't expecting that." I said, being honest. Then, I humped into her and put my hand between her legs, playing in her sex again. I wasn't trying to do no more fucking. I was just enjoying the fact that I was able to touch all on her pussy. I'd grown up looking at her as a mother figure. She'd even given me whoopins before. So, I felt like I was getting away with something.

She laughed. "I feel you getting hard again. You better calm down. Whitney should be on her way home any minute from the club. We can't have her catch us like this or its gon' go down." She scooted forward then stood up, bending over to pick her gown up off the floor, bussing that pussy wide.

I leaned forward so I could sniff the air around that ass, and that made her laugh again, but I was serious. "I hope you know I ain't trying to make this no one time thing. Now that you gave me a shot, I gotta have exclusive access to that body; you understand me? C'mere."

She nodded and walked over to my side of the bed. "Oh, you just thinking you running things now, huh? Like anything you say goes?" She sucked on her bottom lip, looking sexy as hell. Then she took her left hand and rubbed all over my stomach muscles before moving down to my pipe, taking it in her hand and squeezing it. "You are blessed, child. You ain't gotta worry about me saying no. I need all this dick from time to time. We just gotta be careful, that's all I'm saying." She leaned down and kissed the head.

I took my hand and placed it between her legs, rubbing around in her creases, then slid two fingers up her womb and sucked them into my mouth, slurping on them loudly.

"Umm, you so nasty." She took a step back and pulled her gown down. "I got a job today working with Mr. Jones at the funeral home. I'll be in charge of doing the cremations like I used to. That, and some of the makeup. He gon' pay me twelve dollars an hour. I know it ain't much, but it should help with a few of the bills around here. I ain't trying to place all my burdens on your shoulders; please never think that. I already feel weird with having you step in and do all that you are. But I love you for it, and I mean that with all of my heart."

I sat up in the bed, still tasting her pussy on my tongue. I looked her over and smiled. "Yo, it's good, Janet. I know what I gotta do, and you best believe that I ain't got no problem doing it. We're family, and that's what family do. When life gets crazy, we're supposed to bond together and figure it out as one unit. Right now, Nico is down, so it's for me to step up to the plate and make sure that everybody is good, which is why I'm about to hit the ground running. I don't want you feeling like you're a burden to me, because you're not. I love you, and I love Whitney. Y'all are my people, so is Nico." I stood up, walked over to her and hugged her, kissing her on the forehead.

She wrapped her arms around my waist and exhaled loudly.

"I know you miss him, so I'mma do whatever it takes to get him home. I promise you."

Just then, I heard the front door open, and then slam shut. We broke apart, and Janet did the best she could to run out of the room without breaking her neck.

As soon as she got into the hallway, I closed the door, walked over and sat on the bed with my head down. I felt like I had the weight of the world on my shoulders. I didn't know which way to go first. All I saw was the finish line and I knew I had to get to it, and across it by any means. I had a lot of people depending on me, including my own mother. Over the years, me and Nico had accrued a bunch of enemies because of how we got down, and I would be lying to say that it didn't bother me that he wouldn't be by my side as I hit up the slums of Philly, but I had to make do without him, until I was able to get my nigga sprung from that prison.

I bounced off the bed, went into the bathroom, and started the shower all over again so I could cleanse myself. After that, it would be time to get on the grind of my life.

Chapter 4

I had this cousin from New York by the name of Naz, who I jammed with whenever I wasn't joined at the hip with Nico. One of the reasons I fucked with Naz was because he was a pure hustler and got that dough by any means. He was also trigger-happy just like myself, and another reason he'd left behind New York to reside in Philly was because he had a large body count back there. I never got the specifics and I ain't need 'em. Since Nico was down for the moment and I knew I had a bunch of enemies all throughout Philly, I felt it was in my best interest to link up with my cousin and try and put him up on some serious paper.

It was eight o'clock in the morning, the same day that I'd bussed down Nico's mother, and I found myself sitting at Naz's dining room table, while his baby's mother, Shawn, bounced his son on her hip, trying to get the kid to stop crying.

The noise was giving me a headache and I wanted to tell her to take my lil' cousin into another room, but I ain't feel like it was my place to do so. Besides, that would have been rude as hell. I could tell that she was already exhausted and at her wit's end. She had bags under her eyes, and her reddish-brown hair was all over the place. I mean it didn't take away from the fact that she was cute or nothin', it's just that day wasn't one of her better days.

She held the back of the baby's head and rolled her eyes. "Come on, baby, please stop crying." She said with a hint of frustration in her voice that made me feel sorry for her.

"Yo, Shawn, what's taking my cousin so long?" I asked, about ready to go and wait in my Chevy. I'd already been waiting on Naz for about thirty minutes.

She turned her back to me and continued to bounce him. She had on some real lil' yellow shorts that were all up in her ass, so much so that both of her caramel cheeks were exposed on each side. I felt bad for looking but couldn't help it. "Let me go and see what he doing. He said he was finna get in the shower about fifteen minutes ago, but you already know how he is." She said, exhaling loudly.

Shawn and I went to high school together. When we were in the tenth grade, we dated for about four months, then I went and stayed with my old man out in New York. When I came back, we were both different, so we sort of drifted apart. When Naz came from New York about a year before this day, we'd run into Shawn and a few other females at a local club out in Philly, and I introduced them. They'd been together ever since. Naz told me that he'd taken Shawn's virginity, and that she'd gotten pregnant the first time they fucked. He was sick over that fact, and I didn't know why because she was a good girl.

I adjusted my Three Fifty-Seven revolver on my hip and rolled my head around on my shoulders. My stomach began to growl, and I felt a lil' dizzy. I knew I had to put something in my stomach soon.

Shawn came back into the dining room. "Here he come now, and you know he had to curse me out first." She said, still bouncing my lil' cousin.

I scanned her from head to toe real quick and ended up trapped in her hazel eyes. She blushed and looked off, just as Naz came into the dining room with his shirt off, and had two Forty Glocks, one on each hip.

He stopped right in front of her and frowned. "Damn, Shawn, take his crying ass back there somewhere before he gives me a migraine. He too damn spoiled; that's his only problem." Naz said shaking his head.

Shawn scrunched her face. "He ain't spoiled, he might have an ear infection. I think I'ma take him in to be seen today, so before you go anywhere, I'ma need you to drop me off. If that's okay with you." She said this without making eye contact with him. She held the back of their baby's head and forced his face into the crux of her neck while he cried.

Naz curled his upper lip. "I ain't got time for that shit today. You can take him tomorrow or something." He rubbed his temples with his eyes closed.

She blew air through her teeth and shook her head. "I gotta take him today. Just give me a few dollars for an Uber, and I'll take it from there." Now she looked up at him and I could see the anger written all over her face. She was a light skinned female with a golden complexion, but her face was red.

Naz shook his head. "I ain't got no cash right now, but when I get it, you'll get it. Now, take yo' ass in the back while I conduct this business unless you want me to fuck you up. I ain't playing neither." He took a step toward her, and she took two steps back.

Seeing that made me want to say something or intervene, but I had to stay in my lane. My cousin was a looney tune, and I ain't feel like getting into it with him over his woman. I had to get my bands up, so I needed him.

He pointed to the back of the house. "Bitch, go! Now!"

Shawn slowly backed out of the room. "I told you about calling me a bitch in front of our son, Naz. That ain't cool." She said before disappearing.

Naz watched her retreat, and then looked over to me with a mug on his face. "Fuck you doing over here all early and shit? I just went to sleep a few hours ago." He said sitting down at the table across from me.

I reached in between my legs, took the Ziploc bag with twenty thousand dollars' worth of heroin in it, and sat it on the table. "That's twenty gees worth of Boy. I'm trying to get my feet wet in one of the traps. You work beside me I'll give you thirty dollars off every hunnit we make."

He grabbed the bag of dope, pulled it in front of him, stuck his hand into the Ziploc and pulled out a foiled pack. Then he opened it and scooped up a nice portion with his pinky nail and tooting it. He did the same thing with the other nostril. I watched his eyes roll around in his head, then he smiled and began to nod. "Aww, yeah. That's nice right there. It feels like that Haitian tar they got out in DC. We can definitely make some cheese off this. We gon' post up with my lil' niggas on the Ave. They just moved over from New York, and they got their trap jumping like LeBron. It's good. I got history with the lil' niggas, and they loyal. We all stayed in the same projects out in the Bronx." He stood up and pushed the bag back over to me. "Let me go and get dressed then I'll be right with you." He walked out of the dining room.

As soon as he got to the back of the house, I could hear him arguing with Shawn, and then there was a loud slapping sound.

Seconds later, she appeared in the dining room holding her face. Their son was now screaming at the top of his lungs. "I'm tired of this shit." She said with tears rolling down her cheeks. "I wish you never introduced me to his ass, Jayden. He make me wanna kill my-fucking-self, I swear to God." She hugged her son and looked into my eyes.

I shook my head before going in my pocket and pulling out five one hundred-dollar bills. I looked over her shoulder and saw that their bedroom door was still closed. I got up, walked over to her and tried to hand her the money. "Here. This five hundred. Take this money and make sure my lil' cousin get to the doctor today. That shit ain't cool with what he on, but you know I can't get in the middle of that right now. But I' here for you whenever you need me. You got my word on that. You got my number, right?" I asked, handing her the money. The screaming from my lil' cousin made me feel like going insane.

She nodded. "Yeah, I got it, and you sure I can use it?" She asked looking into my eyes once again.

I don't know what it was about Shawn, but whenever she looked me directly in the eyes, she made me feel some type of way. It had been one of the reasons I had been so crazy about her back in the day. That and the fact that she was so demure and fine.

I nodded. "Yeah, you can use it whenever you need it, and I'll do my best to be there for you, aight?"

She smiled and nodded. "Aight, but remember you said that." She took the money, stuffed them into her bra, and walked out of the dining room with her ass cheeks jiggling.

I couldn't do nothing but shake my head.

* * *

I kneeled and placed ten foiled packages in the middle of the two dope fiends and watched as they got their works together.

The skinny, dark skinned sista with a bad wig on top of her head tied the rope around her arm using her teeth, then she smacked at her inner forearm, trying to produce the faint vein that was there. "Come on, bitch. Pop up. I need you right now."

She licked her crusty lips, and as soon as the vein appeared she held her arm out for her girlfriend— a chubby, light skinned woman with a small afro— to draw up the dope from one of the packages, before taking the syringe and sticking the needle into her friend's vein and pushing the feeder downward until the poison slowly entered into her system. I watched her eyes roll back into her head.

She moaned. "Unn, hell yes."

When the heavy-set woman pulled the needle out of her, she prepared it for herself. "Aight, girl, now put this muthafucka in me. You gotta use this vein right here." She said, slapping the side of her neck. I saw a real thick vein appear though it looked a little purple, no doubt from the constant use of it by her. She handed the syringe to her friend and held her head to the side as she injected her.

Naz tapped me on the shoulder. "Bruh, that nigga need five right there, and that white bitch need eleven. Muhfuckas already saying how fire that boy is. That's a good thing."

I walked around the trap, serving one fiend after the next, trying my best to hold my breath and failing. It smelt so bad in there that I was getting sick. Naz acted like the smell didn't bother him at all, and that blew my mind because there was a strong scent of fish, musty under arms, sweat, ass, and dirty pussy all in the air. With the scents being mixed together, it caused for a disgusting concoction that I don't ever think I could've gotten used to. But I kept on serving and filling my pockets with money, and the fiends kept coming, all day and night long.

At about two in the morning, Naz finally shut down shop because we had sold out. I couldn't believe that in a matter of hours I'd made twenty thousand dollars. I gave him six gees and put the rest in one bundle inside of my briefs that I'd worn strictly for that occasion.

Naz walked all around the trap and made sure that all the windows and doors were locked, before he came and plopped down on the couch that was in the middle of the living room. I chose to stand because that couch was funky. It smelled like the dope heads, and I wasn't with that scent.

He sucked his teeth. "I wish you would have saved me a few of them foils, kid. I'm feeling my sick come on." He jerked his shoulders. "Before we turn in, I'ma need a few of 'em, and don't worry, I'ma make sure I hit you for whatever amount of the product that I shove up my nose. I got this shit under control. I understand that it's about the money first and foremost." He pulled on his nose and sniffed the snot back into it.

I nodded. "I got you, kid. It ain't no thang, long as you know what it is. I got a lot of people on my back right now. I can't fall into whatever you got going on with this tootin' shit. How did you get hooked on to this shit anyway? I remember when you first came from New York, you was hollering that Five Percenter stuff. Talking about you had a God body. What made you start putting this poison in it?" I asked, holding my nose. The scent of them fiends were wafting up my nostrils and I was starting to feel sick all over again. I needed to get out of that trap before I threw up all over that dirty ass carpet that looked like everybody had stomped their muddy shoes out on.

Naz wiped his mouth with his right hand and shrugged. "Life happens, kid. Before I left New York, I had to snuff one of my main niggas and his bitch. I grew up with them, and their murders been fucking with me ever since. Then, when I got here, I got Shawn ass pregnant, and truth be told, I ain't ready for no kids, man. I know I'm living on borrowed time and I'm cool with that. I think it was a huge mistake for me to put a baby in her, but that pussy so good, I couldn't help it." He stopped, went into his shirt pocket and pulled out a Newport short and lit it. He inhaled the smoke deeply before blowing it out. "I ain't hit that pussy ever since she had my son. I just don't look at her the same, and I know it's because I'ma fail her and that kid." He took another pull from the cigarette. "I know that for a fact." He stood up and stretched his arms over his head, then started to scratch his stomach. "I'm hungry."

I felt my stomach growling just as well, but the last thing I could think about was food while I was in that stanking ass Trap house. It also bothered me a lil' bit about what he'd said about Shawn. I couldn't believe he wasn't hitting that. There would've been no way I would have been able to stay away from her fine ass. Her body was cold, even after the baby. She had been one of the finest girls in our high school back in the day. It had been one of the reasons I'd gotten at her in the first place. Knowing that he wasn't hitting that pussy intrigued me. I mean, I didn't know if I would have crossed those lines with her or anything like that, but I wasn't ruling it out. I had a thing for thick ass women, and she most certainly fit that bill.

I walked toward the front of the house. "Well, let's go get something to eat, cuz. The smell of this muhfucka making me sick on the stomach. Word is bond." I took the two by four off the door and then unlocked it, pulling it open just a tad. The fresh air coursed into the apartment, and I inhaled it slowly.

Naz picked up the couch that he'd been sitting on, reached under it and came up with a five-shot automatic shotgun, with the pistol grip handle. "Yeah, let's go and get some cheese steaks. Besides, I wanna run something by you anyway." He grabbed his coat off the arm of the couch and put it on before concealing the shotgun inside of it.

Ten minutes later, we were sitting in the parking lot of Mystro's Philly Cheese Steaks and Italian Beefs, trying to get our order together. Mystro's was one of the only restaurants out in Philly that stayed open all night long, and it was cool because they had some of the best food in the city. They were hood yet very professional and clean.

I took out a fifty-dollar bill and turned to Naz. "Yo, so you want two steaks and some cheese fries? And what kind of soda pop?" I was ready to get the food and get back into my car. I was hungry and tired. I couldn't help imagining my bed back at Janet's house.

"Kid, get me one and one, and a Sprite. That way I can hook my shit up when I get back to the crib. Word is bond, I'm trying to lean all night until the morning. You know, before Shawn get to getting on my nerves and shit." He shook his head.

I hopped out of the car and into the night. It was just starting to drizzle a lil' bit, but not enough to drench me, so I was cool with that. I had on a black and gray pair of leather Timb's, and I felt good about my decision to change out of the suede ones I was going to put on before this pair, because the rain would have fucked them up. I popped my hood over my head and stepped into the restaurant's foyer.

There were only two other people inside of it, both females. Well, that was as far as I could tell from behind them. When I stepped in, the door slammed behind me and that made both women turn around to face me. I recognized Jazz's pretty face off the back, and that made me smile.

She lowered her eyes and looked me up and down, stepping to the side as I stepped up to the window to give the cashier my order. I knew we'd made eye contact, but I wasn't go say shit to her right away. She was already bad and shit, and probably used to niggas sweating her like crazy, but that shit wasn't in my DNA. So, I ordered my food then turned my back to her, looking out at the street that Mystro's was located on because the whole hood was known for Stick Up Kids.

I heard one of them suck their teeth loudly, and then they began to whisper amongst themselves before a throat was cleared loudly.

"So, Jayden, you gon' act like you didn't see me when you walked in here?" Jazz asked, coming over and standing on the side of me.

I pulled the hood to my Marc Jacobs back and faced her with a smile on my face. "Aw, I was gon' say something. I was just picking the right time, that's all." I said looking her up and down.

She had on a quarter length Burberry jacket with some tight Burberry pants, over red bottomed Louboutin heels. She slapped her hand on her hip and rolled her eyes. "Really?"

Her friend cleared her throat loudly. "Damn, Jazz, ain't you gon' introduce me to this fine ass nigga?" She asked licking her lip. Then, she bumped Jazz out of the way. "That's okay." She extended her hand. "How are you doing? My name is Stormy, and I think you're fine as hell. Are you looking for a baby mama?" She gave me a look that said she was every bit of serious.

I laughed and shook my head. "N'all, ma, I'm too busy trying to get my life in order. Maybe later though." I said looking over her shoulder at Jazz.

Stormy was about 5'6", high yellow with light freckles all over her face. I couldn't really tell what her body looked like because she had on a long Fendi jacket, but her side profile revealed a nice bump in the ass department.

"It's nice to meet you, Stormy, but I'm trying to see what's good with lil' mama right there." I nudged her just a lil' bit and walked in front of Jazz, looking down on her. "What's good, Play Girl? When you gon' give me some of your time so we can get this money together?"

She looked up at me and smiled, popped back on her legs, then stepped forward and hugged me. "I'm down to do that as soon as possible. What about tomorrow?"

I nodded and looked into her pretty eyes. "That sound good to me. Probably later in the night. You know, after I get done trapping a lil' bit, like nine or something. That sound good to you?" I asked, hugging her, and then breaking our embrace, but not before I caught a whiff of her perfume. She smelt great.

"That sound good to me. You just make sure that you stand on your word and get at me." She patted my chest and laughed.

Stormy walked over and alongside me. "Look, I know you and her got whatever going on, but can I at least get a hug? I ain't seen a nigga as fine as you in a long time." She opened her arms and stepped forward.

I pulled her into my embrace and wrapped my arms around her. She smelled just as good as Jazz, though I could detect a hint of sweat like she'd been dancing or something. I hugged her for a few second, looked over her shoulder at Jazz, and saw her roll her eyes more than once, so I figured it would have been in my best interest to let Stormy go. I wasn't trying to mess things up with Jazz before I even had a chance to get them started. So, I released her and took a step back.

They called Stormy's ticket, so she went to the window to pick up her and Jazz's food.

I looked down on Jazz. "Where y'all coming from? The club or something?" I was curious because it was damn near three something in the morning and I noted specks of glitter all over their faces.

She smiled. "Something like that. We're dancers. We dance at club Oasis up the street. Why you ask me that?"

I shook my head. "No reason, just wondering." I looked into her eyes and she blushed.

Stormy came over with their food. She shook her head at me. "I still can't believe how fine you are. You gotta be mixed with all type of shit, huh?"

I shrugged. "All I know is that my mother is Black. I don't know my pops' ethnicity, so your guess is as good as mine."

"Damn. Can I get one more hug, though? Fa real, and you gotta come by the club some time. I'll give you a few dances for free." She opened her arms and began to walk toward me again with their bag of food in one of her hands.

Jazz grabbed her arm. "N'all, bitch, that's enough. Damn, don't you see us talking?" She asked with her upper lip curled.

Stormy frowned. "Okay. I ain't know it was that serious. I mean, yo' nigga only been on lock for what now? Two months? Already you open for business? Bitch, please." She rolled her eyes and started to walk toward the exit. "I'll meet you back at the club."

I watched her walk out of the door and into the night. It looked as if it was starting to rain a little harder.

Jazz took a deep breath and exhaled slowly. "One day, that bitch gon' make me kill her ass. I don't give a fuck if she my cousin or not." She shook her head. "Anyway, I'll see you tomorrow. In fact, I'm looking forward to it." She hugged me, then took a step back, looking into my eyes before throwing her hood up over her head and running out into the night, just as they called my ticket number.

I grabbed our food and made my way back to the parking lot, but as soon as I got out of the door and looked toward my car, I almost had a heart attack.

Chapter 5

I stepped out into the pouring rain as I watched Naz take the loaded shotgun and stick it into the window of the money green BMW. He cocked it and got to hollering out orders that I couldn't quite make out from where I was.

I jogged over to my car and got behind the wheel, started it up and put it in reverse while I kept my foot on the brake. I didn't know what he was up to, but like I said before, Naz and I were a lot alike. So, if he had a shotgun stuck inside of somebody's car, it had to be for a good reason.

Now that I was closer, I could hear everything that he was saying. "Son, I told you to never come back to Philly, right? I said that if I ever caught you back on this land that I was gon' snuff you. That's what I said right?" He hollered into the passenger's window. I saw him moving around a lot inside the car as if he was choking the person out. I couldn't really see who he was talking to because his big body was blocking the entire opening of the window.

"Yo, I ain't on shit, kid. I came over here to make a drop off, then I'm back out of the city. That's my word!" I heard the victim holler.

"Nah, nigga. I said if I ever saw you again, it was lights out. Matter of fact, what you got in this muhfucka? Hand me the merch!" He hollered, opening the passenger's door and kneeling on the seat. I saw that the barrel of his shotgun was pressed up against a heavy-set, brown skinned nigga's cheek, while he ran his hand all along the man's waist until he came up with a Three-Eighty pistol. He put that on his waist and kept on searching him. "Get yo' bitch ass out of the whip. Now, nigga!"

I looked all around noting that the parking lot was empty and praying that nobody pulled up. The last thing I needed was to go down for a petty ass robbery, or whatever else Naz had in mind. He needed to hurry the fuck up, was the constant thought going through my mind.

The rain began to come down harder and I watched Naz grab the man out of the car by his hair and fling him over the hood of his BMW.

"Say, man, don't do this shit with my son in the backseat. This ain't cool, Naz. You gotta let that shit go." He said, trying to look over his shoulder at Naz.

Naz took his head and slammed his face into the hood of the car so hard that he put a dent in it. "Bitch nigga, shut the fuck up and stay still. I don't give a fuck about that lil' nigga in that backseat. You better have something in this bitch that'll allow him to keep his life, 'cuz if you don't, I'm bodying his ass too. I hope you know that." He went in all his pockets so fast that I was shocked. He pulled out a bundle of cash and stuffed it into his own pockets before turning the man around, so he could face him.

I was so glad that the parking lot was located in the back of the restaurant, because had it been in the front I was sure that one of the employees would have reported this event to the authorities.

Naz took a step back and put the barrel of the shotgun up against the man's Adam's apple after cocking it. "Fuck you got in that trunk, bitch nigga? Once again, remember you and your shorty's life is on the line."

The rain poured down onto their heads, causing their clothes to mat to their skins. Lightning flashed across the sky and illuminated the parking lot for a brief second. The April of 2018's showers were in full effect. I continued to search for any potential witnesses, and thankfully there were none.

The heavy-set nigga swallowed as the rain splashed from his broad forehead. "Yo, I got about nineteen zips in the trunk, and twenty bands. You can have that shit, Naz. Just give me a G-pass on this one. Let me skate with my shorty, man. It's his third birthday." The lightning flashed across the sky again before the thunder growled angrily.

Naz frowned. "N'all, nigga, fuck that. You know how the game go. It's kill or be killed. Yo, Jayden, come here, son!" He hollered over to me.

I stuck my head out of the window and into the rain. "What's good, Dunn?" The rain splashed onto my forehead and rolled down the side of my face before dripping from my chin.

"Yo, come open this nigga trunk, B. I need to get in that muhfucka and keep his ass hemmed up at the same time. Hurry up, Kid." He yelled, then turned the big nigga around and slammed his face into the hood of the BMW again.

"Look, its good, Naz, I ain't playing with you, son. The merch is in there. Trust me."

I jumped out of the car and slid into the open passenger's door, and instead of taking the key out of the ignition, I simply pressed the button on the key chain, and the trunk popped right open. "There you go. Now what?" I hollered, looking into the backseat and into the face of the little boy who was sleeping as if there was nothing going on. He was even snoring a lil' bit.

"Shit, that's it. I'll get up with you tomorrow or something, kid. I gotta handle this business. It's been a long time coming."

I jumped back into my car and backed it out of the parking space as I watched Naz usher the man to the back of the car. Once there, he punched him in the face with his left hand, took a step back and pulled the trigger. *Boom.* His round slammed into the heavy-set man's torso, causing him to fall backward, and that's when Naz picked him up and stuffed him into the trunk while he tried to stop him from closing it. I pulled out of the parking lot and went one way, and he went the other. All I could do was shake my head.

* * *

When I got back to Janet's house that night, I was so hungry that as soon as I kicked my Timb's off and washed my hands, I pulled one of the cheese steaks out and tore into it as if I was starving like crazy, and I felt like I was. I set the bag on the living room table, eating in the dark, when suddenly the light popped on, and there stood Whitney in a small pink tank top and pink, lace boy shorts that looked as if they were too small for her by this point.

I turned and frowned with a mouth full of food. "Damn, girl, you scared the hell out of me." I said half-smacking and half-talking.

She smiled weakly and dabbed at her red eyes. "I'm sorry, I-I didn't mean to scare you. It's just little ol' me." She sniffed and brought the snot back into her nostrils. I could tell that she had been crying. She came and sat down at the table, looking across it at me with a sad look written all over her face.

I slid the bag of food across the table toward her. "Here, it's a few Italian Beefs in there and another cheese steak if you want it. They still hot too." I said, smiling back at her.

She shook her head. "N'all, I still ain't got an appetite. I'm missing Lincoln like crazy, and I can't sleep. I'm thinking about taking an Ambien or something, but I'm scared of pills. All them hoes at the club is addicted to pills. I ain't trying to have no habits." She lowered her head. "I feel so weak, Jayden. I don't know what to do." She exhaled and broke into a fit of tears, sobbing loudly, with both of her hands covering her face. She pushed her chair backward and got ready to stand up. I had made my way around the table and popped a stick of gum inside of my mouth.

I pulled her to her feet and wrapped my arms around her, rubbing her back. She couldn't have been taller than 5'3", though she was built just like her mother. I guided her head until it was laying on my chest. "Yo, anything you need, ma', I'm here for you. You ain't gotta feel what you're feeling alone. Do you hear me?" I asked breaking our embrace just a little bit, so I could look into her face. It was wet with tears. A steady stream that ran all the way down to her neck.

"Jayden, I just miss him so much. Then, the police are saying they don't have any leads. I just don't understand how all of that could take place and nobody knows anything. It doesn't make any sense."

She laid her head back on to my chest and began to cry harder while her chest heaved.

While I didn't give a fuck about Lincoln's bitch ass, I didn't like seeing Whitney break down like that. It caused for my throat to feel as if there was a lump inside of it. I didn't understand how much I cared about her until this day. I took a deep breath and shook my head while I held her close to my body. "Whitney, I know it's hard to hear but you have to move on with your life, or you're going to allow that unfortunate situation to kill you just as well, and there are people here that love and need you just as bad as you felt you needed Lincoln. I swear I wish I could take away all your pain. I would do it in a heartbeat." I held her tighter and pressed my lips against her forehead while she sobbed up under me.

"I just miss him so much, Jayden. He was the only man that loved me for me. Nobody will ever feel that way about me again. I'm not good enough. I just hate life right now." She pushed herself away from me and ran up the stairs toward her room, and then I heard the door slam.

I walked to the edge of the steps and looked upward, trying to decide if I should go up there to try and console her. I hated seeing her in that position. It made me feel less than a man.

Before I could make my mind up entirely, Janet appeared at the top of the steps with her silk robe on and started to come down them. She got about halfway to me before she stopped and looked back up. "Jayden, it's cool. Go up there and make her feel better. I can't have my baby doing nothing to herself. She loved that boy way too much. So, do what you gotta do, Jayden, please." She smiled weakly and came all the way down the stairs just to hug me.

I held her for a second and nodded. "Aight, I'll try, but I don't like seeing her like this. I'm just letting you know." I said releasing her. I swallowed and looked up to the top of the stairs, trying to get my mind together.

Janet grabbed my arm and pulled me to her, pecking my lips. "Nico never liked Lincoln anyway. I'm surprised it took him that long to kill that boy. Now I know what's good, but I have to stay in my own lane like my son keep telling me. However, that don't have anything to do with you. It's your job to help her to get over him. You see what I'm saying?" She asked, rubbing my chest. Then, she ascended the stairs and left me in awe because I had no idea that she'd already known that Nico was responsible for killing Lincoln.

I wondered if she knew that I killed his father. A part of me wanted to ask her, and another part of me didn't. I did wonder if Nico had been the one to tell her about the killings or if she was just trying to put pieces of the puzzle together in her own mind. I wouldn't find out the answers to these questions until a bit later.

After she disappeared into her room, I found myself at the top of the stairs outside of Whitney's door, taking a deep breath before knocking on it three times.

"Who is it?" She whimpered. I could hear SZA's voice singing out of the speakers in her room.

"It's me, Whitney. I need to holler at you for a minute. Can you open the door?" I asked with my hand on the knob.

She was quiet for a minute. I could hear a drawer closing, and then the springs of the bed as she appeared to be sitting back on it after moving some things around. "It's open, Jayden. You can come on in."

I turned the knob and stepped into her room. It smelled like Vanilla scented candles. She was sitting on the edge of the bed in just her little shorts and tank top. I tried not to zoom in on her caramel thighs, but it was hard for me.

I closed the door behind me then looked into her red eyes. "How you doing?" I asked, already knowing the answer to that question.

She shrugged as I slid on the bed beside her, put my arm around her waist, kissing her forehead and holding her firmly. "I feel the same, and I wish I could just move on, but I can't. It's not that easy. I'm a very emotional female. I love hard, and once I get attached to a person, it is so hard for me to move on. I've always been this way, and it sucks."

She exhaled loudly then looked up at me. "Why are you here, Jayden. Did my mother send you?" She wiped her tears away from her cheeks and sniffled.

I shook my head. "I'm here because I wanna help you to feel better. I care about you, Whitney, and I hate to see you breaking down like this. I mean, I understand your pain, but it's killing me to see it." I said speaking the honest to God truth. I did not like seeing her like that, and I didn't understand how a lame ass nigga like Lincoln could get her to be so

66

nutty over him. In my opinion, that nigga was lame as fuck and she was bad— jazzy, high maintenance, classy, and fine as hell. I didn't get it. "Tell me what I can do to make you feel better."

She shrugged. "Are you sure my mother didn't put you up to this, because I heard her door open, and her going down the stairs to where you were. Maybe I'm starting to annoy her or something. I could understand if I am. I just feel so weak." She closed her eyes as more tears sailed down her cheeks.

I wiped them away with my thumbs before holding her beautiful face in my hands. "Whitney, stop that, okay? I'm here because I'm concerned about you, that's it. Your mother asked me to check in on you, but that was after I'd already made my mind up to do so on my own. I promise. Now tell me what it's going to take." I rubbed the side of her face with one hand and kissed her forehead. I watched her close her eyes and then smile.

"Would you mind holding me until I fall asleep? I think I just need to feel protected and safe for a night. I missed feeling secure and up under a protective man, so if you would do that for me, I'd be thankful." She looked up at me and smiled weakly.

I smiled. "Yeah, I'll hold you. Come on. Let's lay down." I stood up and watched her crawl across the bed on all fours.

Her boy short panties were stuck all in her ass, so much so that as she crawled across the bed, I could clearly make out the imprint of her pussy between her legs. It looked full and chunky. Her thick thighs jiggled, and I had to look off because I felt my dick growing up along my stomach. Whitney was having some type of an effect on me that I couldn't control.

She got under the silk sheets before pulling them back for me. "Alright, it's kind of hard for you to hold me if you're standing way over there. Kick those pants off and climb on in. I'ma lay on my left side. Hurry up and protect me." She sucked on her bottom lip and lowered her eyes.

I shook my head and unbuckled my Gucci belt, then unbuttoned my pants and slid them off my legs. I felt my dick moving around inside of my boxers, and I saw her eyes go low and peep its movement. She blushed and looked off, acting as if she hadn't seen anything. I laughed to myself and crawled across the bed, until I was laying on my side behind her. I didn't get under the covers at first because I already knew I wasn't gon' be able to contain myself from catching an erection.

As I was trying to pull her back to me, she sat halfway up and looked over her shoulder. "Get under the covers, Jayden, damn. You act like I'ma bite you or something." She sucked her teeth and pulled it all the way back, exposing those caramel ass cheeks again. "Come on."

"Aight." I slid under the covers and pulled them over us. Then I pulled her all the way to me until her ass was in my lap and the back of her head was up against my lips. I inhaled her feminine scent and felt my piece rising. I tried to back away, but that did very little to help the situation. "Look, Whitney, I ain't trying to be bogus or nothin' like that, but you just gotta know that my piece gon' rise because we're in such a close proximity. I ain't trying to come at you reckless or nothing like that. Aight?"

She giggled. "It's good. I mean, I am grown, and I get what happens to a man. I guess I should take that as a compliment, even though I know you see me as your little sister." She scooted back into me and wiggled her ass just a little bit. Her crack was trying to pull my pipe inside of it. At least that's what it felt like.

Instead of moving backward, I scooted forward as I felt him getting super hard. I picked up her leg and put it back down so that it trapped my pipe between her thighs. Somehow, he'd made his way out of my boxer hole.

"You feel that?" I asked, kissing the back of her neck before nipping at it with my teeth.

She moaned. "Yeah. It's so hard. You telling me I got you feeling like that? I thought all you saw was Nico's little sister. I never thought you noticed me." She whispered, leaning her head forward so I could attack that neck.

I scooted further into her, took my hand and ran it all over her stomach before trailing it down to the hem of her boy shorts. I slid my fingers inside of them, but then took them down to her pussy, even though she opened her legs wide for me. "You're bad, Whitney, and I don't want you hurting no more. It's my job to protect you now that Nico's gone, and I'ma do that by any means. You hear me?" I moved my hand all the way down and slid my fingers into the crease of her slippery pussy.

"Unnn, Jayden." She moaned and opened her legs wide before laying on her back. She pulled me down by my neck and kissed my lips, sucking all over them. "I need to get over him, Jayden. I need you to help me, big bro. Please. We ain't gotta have sex, just touch me. Please, touch me." She licked my lips and slid her tongue into my mouth, humping into my hand.

I was playing with her juicy pussy now—opening the lips and sliding two fingers deep into her center, while my thumb ran circles around her clitoris. I started fingering her nice and slow, but within seconds it was fast paced with her hips humping off of the bed and onto them. She opened her mouth wide as tears slid down her cheeks.

"It's okay, baby. Cry. Get them tears up out of your system." I coaxed, adding a third finger into her soaking wet box.

I'd never seen a pussy so wet in my entire life at. It was so wet that there was a large puddle up under her ass. Man, it took everything in me not to climb on top of her and fuck the shit out of her, but I had to keep in mind that it wasn't about me. It was about her.

"Un, un, un, un, Jayden, it feel so good. Finger me. Unnn, baby, finger me harder. I need it." She cried, opening her legs wider.

I started to finger her so fast that my bicep on my right arm was bulging out of my shirt. Her legs were in the air. Her pretty toes were pointed toward the ceiling while her eyes were closed tight. "Cum for me, lil' sis. Cum for me. It's okay, baby. It's okay. I know what you need. Let me see you cum as hard as you can." I went as fast and as hard as I could, watching her face scrunch up.

"Uhhh! Uhh! I'm cumming, Jayden. I'm cumming for you. Uhh, thank youuuu-a!" She moaned before shaking on the bed.

As soon as she started to cum, I hurried and put my face between her legs, sucking her clit into my mouth while my teeth nipped at it again and again. She squirted into my mouth, moaning at the top of her lungs as SZA played in the background.

Afterward, I laid on my back and pulled her on top of me, so I could rub all over that fat ass booty. I did feel some type of way about just having ate my right-hand man's sister's pussy, especially after he'd told me specifically to stay away from her, but that night I felt like she needed me, and I hoped he would have understood that.

Whitney climbed up my body and laid her head on my chest, while I continued to rub all over that booty. It felt soft and hot. I couldn't believe how fat it really was until I got to squeezing it, loving the feel of it.

"Jayden, I hope you don't look at me all weird and stuff because I let you do that. I just really needed to escape the pains of my heart, and I'm thankful for what you just did. But it can't ever go any further than that, okay?" She asked, kissing my chest, and then looking into my eyes. There were a few tear streaks along her cheeks.

I nodded. "Yeah, I get that, and I can respect what you're saying. Just know that I'm always gon' be there for you whenever you need me to be. We ain't gotta put no stipulations on this. I got you, no matter what." I slid my fingers into her ass crack, and rubbed them down on to her wet, hot pussy lips, before separating them, and sliding my middle finger back into her tight lil' hole.

She arched her back and sat down on my finger with her eyes closed. "You betta stop 'fore you get us in trouble. What you think Nico gon' do if he found out how you got me in this bed right now? You know he'll go ballistic. After all, you're like my second big brother." She kissed my chest and got up from the bed, putting a robe around her sexy body.

I caught one last glimpse before it disappeared, causing my pipe to jump. She saw it and laughed.

I sat up. "We ain't gotta worry about what Nico would think 'cuz we ain't did nothing, and the lil' that we did do is our lil' secret. I did what I had to, to make you feel better. Nah'mean?"

She walked over to the bed, climbed across it on her knees before straddling me and pushing me backward so she could lay her head on my chest. "I know, Jayden, and I love you for it."

Chapter 6

I popped the cork on the bottle of Ace of Spades after picking up Jazz's champagne glass, then I filled it halfway before grabbing mine and doing the same thing. It was the next night, and after trapping the entire day alongside Naz, Jazz had hit me up saying that she wanted to meet for drinks over at Emilio's, which was a nice, laid back four-star restaurant located right off the Avenue. I took her up on her request and got there as soon as I could.

She took the champagne glass and took a sip from it. "So, Jayden, what's your deal? What would make you come at me the way you did? I know you saw my man right there, but that didn't stop you. What's up with that?" She asked setting her glass down and smiling over at me.

I took a sip from my glass, swishing the liquid around in my mouth before swallowing it. "I see what I want, and I go and get it. You caught my attention as soon I saw you, so I had to have you. That's just what it is. That nigga will be aight."

She frowned and moved her glass to the side, so she could lean forward. "Oh, so you think you got me? Well, let me tell you something. Don't no nigga got me. I got me. All this is, is a formal business arrangement whether you know it or not. So, you can get your head out of the clouds." She rolled her eyes and sat back in her seat as the waiter came and set two steaming plates of triple cheese lasagna on our table before walking away in silence. She took her big napkin, opened it and placed it over her lap, mugging me from across the table.

I looked at her for a long time and grunted. "What's the attitude about? Seems like you're overreacting about what I said to you. Shit ain't that serious." I grabbed my napkin and opened it, putting it across my lap like I saw her do. I never had before, but I figured it was what you did when you went to a halfway decent restaurant. I was a street dude and ate mostly fast food. Me sitting down at a four-star restaurant didn't happen too often, and I was starting to regret it already.

Jazz took one of her curly locks and tucked it behind her ear. "I just hate when a man feels like he's taken ownership of me in one way or the other. My whole life I've been dealing with that type of shit and I'm tired of it. Nobody owns me, and nobody has me. I'm my own woman and I stand on my own two feet. Let's get that perfectly clear out of the gate, that way we won't have any serious issues. You feel me?" She looked over and into my eyes, waiting for my response.

I nodded, and for some reason I was feeling her even more because of how she was coming at me. She seemed strong, like one of those women that were going to make me fight hard to break her ass down, because that was definitely the game plan. The harder she made me work, the more intrigued I would become, until ultimately, I conquered her ass. I couldn't wait. But for the moment I was going to play my role. "Yeah, that's my bad, Jazz. I don't know what you've been through, but it sounds like a lot. Let me start over." I took a sip from the champagne. "I saw you, you looked real good to me, so I had to see what was good. The fact that you had a man ain't mean shit to me. I got a problem with boundaries anyway." I said truthfully.

She nodded and dug into her lasagna, cutting it with her fork before scooping a nice portion into her mouth, and chewing. "I did my research on you, Jayden. You know the streets talk, and from what I hear out in Philly, you're one of them niggas." She had moved the food into one of her jaws while she said what she said. I thought that was kind of cute because here she was, this fine ass female, all made up, looking classy, but talking with a mouthful of food.

"Oh, the streets talk, huh? Yeah, well, what they saying about me?" I took a hunk of my lasagna and forked it into my mouth, chewing with my eyes closed. Lasagna was my favorite food, and Emilio's knew how to throw down. I sipped my drink.

Jazz dropped her fork and wiped her mouth on the napkin as the jazz band played in the background about twenty feet away on stage.

Even in the dim light of the restaurant, I couldn't help but to acknowledge how fine this woman was sitting across from me. Every time I looked into her eyes it got me excited.

"I hear you about that life. That you and your mans Nico don't take no shit from nobody. That y'all done ran a few niggas out of Philly, back to New York and D.C. That you been popped a few times, and so has your cousin, but you niggas won't die."

Now, I was feeding my face and enjoying my meal. I nodded. "And, so how that make you feel?"

She sucked on her bottom lip and picked up her champagne glass. "Like I'm talking to the right man for what I got in mind." She closed her eyes and sipped out of her glass.

I took a second and trailed my eyes down to her C-cup titties. They were pressed up against her Prada dress, and the middle of the dress was left open, so she could show off her ample cleavage. She looked good, and I had to have that. At the same time, I wanted to hear what she was getting at.

"Let me hear what you got on your mind." I wiped my mouth on my napkin and looked across the table at her.

She curled her upper lip. "Like I said before, I'm tired of men that think they own me in some form or fashion, and I'm ready to clap back at they ass, and hit 'em where it hurts. Right in their muthafuckin pockets. I got some things up my sleeve that I think you'll be perfect for carrying out. I mean, since the streets already bow down to your gangsta." She looked me in the eyes again, then smiled weakly.

"How much money we talking? And secondly, how soon can we get shit kicked off? I got obligations in the slums." I said, matching her intense stare.

She sucked her teeth. "If we do shit right, and you allow for me to set things up the way they're supposed to be, I don't see us making less than fifty thousand each time, and I'm talking that's a minimum, but we should make more than that. What it is, is I have a few girls that run under me that have these high-paid tricks that I'ma need you to hit when I say hit them. Some of the licks will be hustlers out here in Philly. Some may be well-off businessmen, and there may be sometimes that you'll have to travel outside of the city to buss a move. But each time it'll be well worth it. I'll be able to provide you with a full blue print of each operation. All you'll have to do is execute and get the fuck out of there. We'll split the money right down the middle, and I'll take care of my girls." She sipped out of her champagne glass. "Seems easy enough, right?"

I was leaning forward with my fingers interlocked. I nodded. "Yeah, so what's the catch?" I knew there had to be one.

She laughed. "Damn, you definitely hip to the streets." She cleared her throat and looked around the restaurant before looking back at me. "Well, there are two things. The first, and I'm willing to pay you fifty bands up front for this alone." She exhaled again and shook her head. "I need for Nico to kill Buns. He's the man you saw me talking to when you approached me in the county jail. Apparently, he ain't cool with me moving on with my life now that he's been put away. He feels that I should shut everything down and put my life on hold for him, and I ain't cool with that. One clown can't stop no show, you feel what I'm saying? But the last time I went to go and see him, he flat out said that he would have me killed if I didn't fall in line, and I believe him, so I need his ass whacked." She sat back in her chair and crossed her legs.

I shrugged. "I go and see my nigga this week and I'll run that by him, but I know it ain't gon' be a problem, especially since we trying to get lawyer money right now. What's the second thing?"

"His baby's mother has his safe at her home. I know it's more than two hunnit gees in it, and that's not counting the dope. I need you to hit her and take the kid and bring him to me. Reason being, Buns got niggas all up and down the east coast that fuck with him the long way. They ain't really killas like you and Nico from what I hear, but they got that paper, and if his son is taken hostage, they'll put up at least a million for his safe return. I don't know about the whole safe return, if you get my drift." She wiped her mouth with her hand and exhaled, looking me in the eyes like an evil killer.

She had so many numbers running through my head that I was with everything she was saying. I didn't give a fuck about Buns, his kid, his baby mother, or none of them. I wasn't into killing a shorty, but for the right price I was sure I would, so I was down for the cause. I had to get my nigga out and we had to get our bands all the way up. I was tired of being broke.

I sat back in my seat and looked her over closely, while she kept her eyes pinned on mine. "Jazz, you do what you gotta do, and I'll handle my end. Don't you worry about that." I leaned forward and rested my elbows on the table, looking her over. "I do got one question for you, and I just want you to keep shit real with me, so we can move forward. Can you do that?"

She laughed and sucked her bottom lip again. I guess that was a habit of hers. I thought it made her look real sexy. "I mean, I ain't gon' say that I don't lie, cheat and steal as you probably figured out, but in this case, yeah, I'll keep shit one hunnit."

"I wanna know what made you come to me about all this. You don't know me from Adam, and you're laying some pretty heavy things into my lap. What gives?"

She scrunched her pretty face. "What? You can't handle it or something?" She looked disgusted.

"Ma, you need to calm yo' ass down. Now, I get that you got a real bad attitude and shit 'cuz you been out here in these streets, and I respect that. But when you fucking with me, you gon' honor my gangsta just as well. Now, why did you choose me?" I felt my blood boiling. It was only so much of that tough shit that I could take at one time. I understood she wasn't the average weak female, and that was cool, but enough was enough.

She smiled and laughed to herself. "Yeah, me and you gon' butt heads a lot, but I look forward to it." She sucked her teeth, and once again scanned the restaurant before looking back into my eyes. "The reason I chose you is because of how you came at me, even with Buns looking right at you. I mean, I know he was behind the glass and all that, but that wouldn't stop him from having you knocked off. I felt like you just didn't give a fuck. Then, when I ran your name through Philly's version of Google, I got the impression that you didn't take no shit from nobody, and like I said, you're about that life, so I figured why not? The slums are about taking risks, so that's what I'm doing." She ran her tongue over the top row of her teeth. "Any more questions, or can we get this show on the road?"

I laughed. "Just get your ducks in a row and get at me. I'm ready whenever you are. Trust me on this."

* * *

A couple days later, I was in the hot ass visiting room of the prison where Nico was being held. It was so hot in that muhfucka that I was sweating like I'd just got done playing a game of basketball. Not only was the heat getting to me, but I think it was also the fact that I didn't like being inside of nobody's prison. I'd always said that I'd rather make the police kill me with their guns than with their handcuffs. Meaning that I'd rather for them to shoot me down in the streets instead of taking me into custody and making it so that I died in one of their slammers. I just didn't have that shit in me. So, as I waited for Nico to come out, I was sweating bullets, dabbing at my forehead with a paper towel.

He came through one of the doors about thirty minutes later, and by that time I'd struck up a conversation with a thick ass dark skinned female, who had a little boy sitting on her lap that looked to be about the age of four. She'd made it seem like she knew me from somewhere, and when I told her that she didn't, she shrugged and asked me what was good anyway. Before I could get all her information, her baby's father had come out right in front of Nico.

I got up and gave the homey a hug and felt him wrap his arms around me. "What's good, Boss? How you been holding up in this muhfucka?" I asked before releasing him. I noted that the dark skinned sista tongued her baby daddy down before they sat down. I laughed to myself and shook my head before sitting across from Nico.

He sat all the way on the edge of his gray, plastic chair. "Bruh, where my moms at? Ain't nothin' wrong with her is it?" He asked looking worried. He had already begun to sweat.

I shook my head and handed him a bunch of paper towels. "N'all, she good. I told her that I needed to holler at you on my own today and she damn near killed me to prevent that from happening. Long story short, all the bills are paid up. It's plenty food in the house, and I'm finna run some shit by you that's gon' help you get a lawyer like ASAP. It's just a lil' bit a business that you gotta take care of on the inside here. You cool with that?" I asked, feeling a bit of sweat roll down my neck. I was uncomfortable as hell, and the air was as thick as a peanut butter sandwich.

"Son, for lawyer money, I don't give a fuck what I gotta do, that shit is done. Word is bond." He wiped his forehead. "Yo, it's hot as a bitch in here." He turned all the way around and faced the desk where there were four correctional officers. "Say, CO? Why don't y'all turn the air conditioner on in this muhfucka, man? It's kids in here!" He hollered with a mug on his face.

There was a short, fat white man, balding, that threw his arms in the air. "It's broken. Maintenance won't be out 'til Monday morning. It sucks, we know."

Nico waved him off. "Punk ass Crackers probably doing that shit on purpose. I hate these bitches. Word to my mother."

I laughed and nodded. "Yo, I feel you, kid, but chill out before they try and throw you in the hole or some shit. Peep game." I wiped my forehead again and tried to breathe easy. "Yo, it's a nigga here by the name of Buns, right? He should've came on the same bus you came down on a few weeks back."

Nico nodded. "Yeah, big, fat, dark skinned nigga, from DC, but moved out to Philly about two years ago. I'm familiar. What's good with him?" He asked, curling his upper lip.

"You gotta bag son. I don't give a fuck how you do it, long as kid ain't got no life left in him. You body this nigga, and I can guarantee you lawyer money. I want you outta here, kid. I need you back by my side, so handle this nigga."

Nico nodded and scrunched his face. "Who you out there fucking with that want him dead? Fill me in." He wiped sweat from around his neck and got to popping his state top repeatedly to get some air inside of it.

I shook my head. "The less you know, the better. I just need you to trust me on this one. Know that I got your best interest at heart. Yo, I'ma go get a couple juices and some other shit to eat real quick to stop this torture. You want anything in general?" I asked, getting ready to get up and go to the vending machines for the homey. I'd brought in fifty dollars' worth of quarters to make sure he ate as much as he wanted to.

He pointed at my chair. "Fuck that food, kid. You talking about my freedom right now. That shit can wait. I need to know who you fucking with so I can know how deep this shit go with this stud. I mean, he's a dead man walking, but I still just need to know." He wiped his face again.

"This nigga's old bitch got the whole low down on 'em. She's putting up fifty gees for us to body his ass. I'ma take that paper and grab you a lawyer. Then, I got some other shit up my sleeve that should have you coming home to a nice piece of change. You just gotta trust that I got this hit under control."

He shook his head. "N'all, kid, I definitely know you got me. We cut from the same cloth. I just wanted to know where you coming from. You know how it is." He laughed and sat back in his chair. "His bitch, huh?" He shook his head. "They always say that money is the route to all evil, but its most definitely nine times out of ten, a bitch." He nodded and moved to the front of his chair. "I'ma bag this fuck nigga before the week out. You make sure ol' girl have them chips ready or she gon' be the next muhfucka on our hit list. I ain't playin' about my freedom, son, and I already know that you ain't either." He sucked his teeth and looked at the ground with an angry look on his face. "What's good with Whitney? You ain't fucked her or nothin' like that, have you?" He slowly trailed his eyes up from the floor and into mine before lowering them.

Nico was a cold-blooded killer like myself. Whenever I lowered my eyes after asking somebody a question it was because I needed to zone into them with everything I had at that time. I knew how to react against this stare. I just had to remain calm and keep my composure.

"Yo, she been going through a thing over that Lincoln stud, but she getting better. Far as me fucking her, I'd never cross you like that, kid. She's just as much of my little sister as she is yours. It's my job to protect her, even after you get home."

Nico smiled. "That's what I like to hear. I ain't mean no disrespect by that question. I just know how she is when she gets vulnerable. On top of that, she loves real hard, so I can only imagine how that fool's death got her feeling. The last few days that I've talked to her, she's been saying your name more than usual, so that got me to thinking some things, that's all." He wiped his forehead that had filled up with sweat. "Any way it goes, you gotta remain loyal to me, Jayden, and stay away from her. I can tell that she starting to feel some type of way about you, so be careful. I love you like my brother, but on some real shit, I'd kill you over my sister. I'm just keeping that shit one hunnit." He looked deep into my eyes at saying the last part, and I knew he was serious.

I loved my nigga with all my heart, but I didn't like hearing him say that he'd kill me. I didn't give a fuck what circumstance it was under. Hearing him say that shit made me want to be rebellious. He made Whitney become irresistible to me. As soon as those words left his mouth, I started to feen for her on every single level. But once again, I had to play shit cool. So, I smiled and looked into his eyes. "Well, you ain't ever gotta worry about no shit like that. That's our baby sister, and as far as I'm concerned, some lines are never supposed to be crossed. Nah'mean?"

I ran my tongue across my teeth and looked around the visiting room because looking into Nico's eyes were getting me heated. I felt my heart pounding in my chest. Had he not been my right-hand man and had threatened my life like that, I'd a knocked his noodles out of his head and kept it moving. But he was like my blood, so I had to let this one pass for the moment.

Nico laughed to cut the tension in the air. "Anyway, bruh, I got this nigga in here. You handle yo' business out there and we'll be good. I love you, my nigga. Never forget that."

I stood up and we embraced. "Yeah, it's good," I said, patting him on the back. I couldn't even bring myself to return his love because I kept on seeing myself splashing my nigga. I don't know why my brain was set up like it was, but that one comment by him had caused a switch to flip within me, so instead of telling him that I loved him, I said, "I put a gee on your books, too, and I'll make sure your moms get up here on Tuesday. I got you and I got them."

He hugged me tighter before stepping back. "I appreciate you, bruh, fa real. Never forget why I'm here, and who I did this shit for. Nah' mean?" He looked into my eyes again and lowered his head, sucking his teeth loudly.

I nodded. "N'all, I'd never forget that."

We locked eyes and held each other's stare for a few seconds, then a guard came over and stood alongside our table. He looked from me to Nico, and then wiped his forehead that was full of sweat. "You guys done here?"

I nodded, still looking into Nico's eyes. "Yeah, we are."

Chapter 7

The next morning, I got up nice and early, went downstairs and whipped up a nice breakfast consisting of sausage and cheese omelets, with French toast, a bowl of cheese grits, and a glass of orange juice. I put it all on a tray and made my way up the stairs to Whitney's room. The previous night she'd gotten home late, so I knew that she'd still be in bed catching up on her sleep. The strip club that she worked at was obviously wearing her lil' ass out, and I had yet to talk to her about working there. I figured that she maintained her employment there, so she could help with the bills, and I respected that. I didn't like lazy people, and that she was not.

Janet had already left for her gig at the funeral home, so the house was nice and quiet. I stepped up to Whitney's door and tapped on it four times, awaiting her response. When none came, I tapped again, adjusting the tray of food in my hands, situating the red rose that I had laid across the tray, right under the plate of food. Once again, there was no response. All I could hear was the singing of SZA's voice on the other side of the door. I knew that Whitney often fell asleep to SZA. I took a deep breath, leaned on the door and twisted the knob, finding it unlocked before pushing it inward.

As soon as I opened the door, my eyes got bucked, and I felt my heart begin to pound in my chest. There was Whitney, sprawled out on the bed, laying on her stomach with her right leg pushed up to her rib cage. Between her thighs she wore a red G-string that was somehow pulled to the side, exposing her brown, naked pussy lips below, and a hint of the crinkle of her asshole up top. I felt weak in the knees as I stepped further into the bedroom, took the tray of food and set it on the top of her dresser right next to her cell phone. Once I set it down, I turned back around and made my way to her bed while SZA sang on in the background about love galore.

I crawled onto the bed hearing her snore lightly, took my nose and sniffed up and down her crease with my eyes closed, then I leaned forward and sucked her pussy lips into my mouth, along with a portion of the G-string, sending my tongue up and down her slit at the same time to taste her.

"Unnn-a." She moaned, moving her thigh further upward, exposing more of her kitty to my view. Her pretty toes curled before opening again.

I opened her pussy lips and sucked on her clit, flicking it with my tongue, sucking on it, nipping it with my teeth before licking up and down her slit while her juices began to flow out of her. They tasted salty and sweet at the same time.

"Huuh-a, huuh-a, umm-hmm, uh." She moaned, moving her knee all the way to her rib cage, reaching over her waist and pulling her lips apart for me.

That got me to wondering if she was still sleep, or if she knew what was happening and was down with it. Either way, I didn't care because I was going to finish what I started no matter what. The smell of her on my upper lip was driving me crazy. That mixed with the threat from Nico was causing me to yearn for her body in a way that I never had before. I started to attack that pussy, eating like a thirsty lesbian, sucking all over her lips, and nipping at her clit, while she yelped and moaned at the top of her lungs.

Finally, her eyes popped open and she looked back at me. "Jayden, what are you doing?" She moaned, and tried to bring her thick thigh downward, but I prevented that by holding it in my hand, forcing it open further while I sucked all over her sex lips loudly, slobbering and doing my thing. "Un, un, shit! Stop, Jayden! We can't do this. Please." She pulled at the sheets to try and get away from me.

I got to my knees and flipped her onto her back, forcing her knees to her chest and burying my face back between her legs, after spreading her pussy lips and going in on her erect clitoris. It stood out about an inch, just enough for me to trap within my lips while I fingered her at full speed.

"Uh, uh, uh, Jayden, Jayden, uh. What. Are. You. Uhhh-a! I'm cumming! I'm cumming, Jayden! Uhhh-a, fuck!" She hollered, bucking on the bed while I continued to eat that pussy, swallowing her juices and everything.

I was laying on my stomach, and my dick was so hard that I was humping into the bed. The scent of her was getting the better of me.

I tilted my head with her juices all over my face and chin, pulling my Polo pajama pants down by the waistband. "I gotta have some of this pussy, Whitney. I'm feening for you, baby. I need this." I said, kicking my pants off. I was already without boxers, so once they were off I was naked from the waist down.

She kicked at me and tried to push me off. "No, Jayden! We can't. We can't do this. It's not right. I promised Nico." She tried to wiggle from under me, but I wasn't let her go nowhere.

I got between her legs, leaned down and held her arms out to her sides, sucking on her long neck that still smelled like her Fendi perfume. My hard dick throbbed against her mound. Its heat caused my pipe to jump in anticipation.

"Unn, Jayden. Stop, please. You're going to make me hurt my brother. Please, don't. Unn-a!" She moaned, humping her mound into my pipe.

The head went a tad bit inside of her sex lips before slipping out. I started to grind into her, running my dick head up and down her slit, coating it with her juices. I made sure that I bumped against her clit repeatedly until it got to the point that she was humping into me. "You want me too, Whitney. I know you do, baby. Look how wet this pussy is. Just tell me. Tell me you want your other brother. Let me hear it." I sucked on her neck and lined my dick up with her dripping hole.

She pushed at my chest. "No, get off me, Jayden. Please." But at the same time, she wrapped her legs around my waist. "I don't want to hurt Nico. I promised him." She said barely above a whisper. "Unn, shit."

"Aight, then, it's all on me. I'll take the blame. I'll be the bad guy, 'cuz I'm finna take this pussy. Just keep saying no, and this will never be your fault." I wormed the head into her tight hole, cocked back and slammed forward hard, implanting myself deep

90

within her womb, feeling her heat sear me. It felt like my dick was being squeezed by a tight, wet fist.

"Uhhh! Shit, Jayden. There you go. There you go, big bruh." She cried. "Now take this pussy!" She opened her thighs wide.

I put her right ankle on my shoulder and got to fucking her pussy hard; watching my dick go in and out of her. Her lips opened and closed around the thick pole, saturating me with juices from deep within her center. "Give me this pussy! This my shit. This my shit. This my shit. You hear me?" I growled, slamming into her box. I kept on hearing Nico's threat in the back of my mind. And every time I repeated it to myself, it made me fuck Whitney harder and harder.

"Uh, uh, uh, uh, wait, Jayden, please. You're killing me, big bruh. Uhhh-a, you're fucking. Me. So. Hard. Shit!" She screamed. Then there were tears coming out of her eyes. She opened them and looked up at me, vulnerable.

I picked her left ankle up and put it on my shoulder as well, and really got to fucking her like an animal while her titties jiggled on her chest, up under her white beater. I stopped, ripped it down the middle, exposing her breasts, then sucked the first nipple and then the other with the headboard slamming into the wall loudly.

"Uhhh! Jayden, I'm cumming, Jayden! Oooo-a, shit, big bruh! Uhhhh-a!" she screamed, before closing her eyes, and shaking as if she were having a seizure.

At the feel of her cumming, it caused my body to go tight before I felt the tingles in my balls, then I was coming deep within her womb, jerking like crazy, as glob after glob came out of me. With every drop that shot into her I could hear Nico's voice threatening me.

She fell onto her back with tears running down her cheeks. "I need you, Jayden. I need you so bad." she said breathlessly.

I leaned down and kissed all over her juicy lips. "I'm here, baby. It's me and you now. I got you. That's all I want you to know. It's me and you." I growled, feeling my dick harden inside her again. I licked her tears from her face, then kissed all over them before sucking on her neck again.

"What about Nico? He's going to be so mad at me." She whimpered, then broke into a fit of tears.

I flipped her onto her stomach, then got on her back, slipping my dick into her hard before pounding into her guts while I held her right leg in my forearm and sucked on the back of her neck. "Fuck, Nico! I got you! You. Hear. Me!"

"Yes! Yes! I. Hear. You! Please. Jayden, you're fucking. Me like crazy!" she screamed, arching her back as I pulled her hair, taking her hip and forcing her to slam back into me. After a short while she was doing it on her own, loving the dick.

"Tell me you love this dick, Whitney! Tell me! Now!" I hollered through clenched teeth. Her pussy was so good that I was kicking myself in the ass for not coming at her sooner. I popped my back and continued to slam into her, forcing her into submission.

"I love it, Jayden. Ooo-a! I love it. Fuck me harder! Fuck. Me. Harder. Please! I need you!" she cried.

I pulled her up on all fours by grabbing a handful of her hair. Once there, I pushed her face into the bed so that her fat ass booty was in the air and bussed open. The crinkle of her ass hole was glistening with her pussy juices. The juices ran down her inner thigh and to her knee, just as her mother's had. Both women had some good pussy, and the fact that I knew that firsthand made me smile.

I slid back into Whitney, took her hips and forced her back into me again and again. "Tell me. Tell. Me. That you need me!" I growled with our skins slapping together loudly. Our scents were heavy in the air.

"I need you, Jayden! I. Need. You!" she cried before lifting her face and looking back at me with tears in her eyes.

I pushed it back to the bed and smacked her on the ass. "Tell. Me. I. Own. This. Pussy!" I sped up the pace, watching my dick shoot in and out of her, taking my index finger and slipping it into her asshole, moving it in and out.

"Mmmm-a! It's yours! It's yours! Mmmm-a, Jayden!" She took her face from the bed sheets, screaming with her face toward the ceiling and started to cum again.

I kept on clapping that pussy from the back until I couldn't take it no more. I slammed forward five quick times and came so hard, deep within her womb again, that I damn near passed out. The pussy was awesome.

Afterward, I held her in my arms while she rubbed all over my chest and abs. "Jayden, I'm not gon' be able to stop myself from being addicted to you. It's just how I am. How are you going to handle that?" she asked, looking up at me with wide eyes.

I rubbed that fat ass booty and squeezed it. "Long as you know I got you, Whitney, that's all that matters. I want you to be you, and we'll take it from there." I yawned. I was so tired, and knew I had to get up in a few hours so I could meet up with Naz, so we could go trapping.

I didn't know how I truly felt about Whitney at that time. All I knew was that that forbidden box between her legs had me yearning for some more. I did like her, and she was a bad female. I just didn't know if I cared about her, and I knew that I would never let nothing happen to her if I could prevent it. The only problem was that I knew Nico would never accept what had taken place between us, and once he found out he would for sure come for my life. He'd meant every word that he'd said about me messing around with Whitney. I didn't fully understand what his issue was, but a part of me didn't give a fuck. I had to have her. I just didn't know where she would fit into my life's overall plan.

She kissed my chest and rubbed her cheek up against it. "I know you got me, Jayden. You've always tried your best to be there for me and I appreciate that." She sighed. I could feel her hot breath blow against my skin. "I'm just worried about my emotions. They can be a problem for a man to handle once they become so strong. It's one of the reasons I loved Lincoln so much. It was because me being so clingy didn't seem to bother him. That's rare." She looked up and rubbed my cheek. "Am I going to be your woman now?" She traced the contours of my lips with the tip of her index finger.

I continued to rub all over that booty. It felt so soft and hot in my hand. I almost wanted to go for another round but had to be conscious of the fact that she wasn't trying to connect in a sexual way. She needed me more emotionally, so I had to meet her halfway and say some of the things that I know she needed to hear.

I nodded. "If you was my woman, Whitney, I'd take care of you and make sure you never needed for anything. I'd hold you down and try my best to keep you first and above all because that's what you deserve." I leaned down and kissed her juicy lips, feeling her grab the back of my head so our kiss could last longer than I intended for it to.

She broke the kiss and kept her eyes closed, rubbing her chin against my lips. "I've always seen you as another big brother, but I can't lie, I do want to be your woman. I need that kind of love. I'm not a lil' girl anymore."

I scrunched my face as I rubbed all over that ass. "What make you say that, Whitney?"

"No, I just know that you're probably used to seeing me as a little sister, or that little girl that was always so whiney back in the day. I'm just letting you know that I'm not her anymore. That I'm a woman, and if I'm going to be your woman, then you're going to have to treat me as such, because that's what I'll need." She rubbed my chest then looked into my eyes. "Can you do that, Jayden?"

I nodded. "Yeah, I got you, lil' mama? But what about Nico? What if he finds out about you and I? Who you gon' roll with? Keep in mind that he gon' be ready to go all out over you, so I need to know what's good before we go this route." I slid my fingers into her crease and squeezed her kitty lips together, causing a trickle of juice to ooze out. I sucked the finger into my mouth. Damn, she tasted good.

She took a deep breath and sat up with her back against the headboard. Her perfect titties were exposed for my gazing. She looked so damn fine that I couldn't help noticing that. She covered her face with both hands and lowered her head. "I don't know what we're goin' to do about Nico. I promised him that I wouldn't cross lines with you. I swore it on our grandmother's grave, yet here I am. Weak, already." She shook her head. "Typical me." She exhaled loudly again.

I slid out of the bed and picked up my pajama pants before sliding them back on. I looked over my shoulder at her and shook my head. "Well, I guess you got some things to figure out. I mean, I wouldn't want to come between you and your brother and all. That is my mans too, and I guess I should feel as bad as you feel, but I don't. The thing is that I really care about you, Whitney, and I would love for you to be my woman, but I ain't accepting no half-stepping. If you gon' be mine, then you gon' ride and die for me, just like I am for you. You hollering you ain't no lil' girl no more, but you still scared of your older brother, allowing for him to make your decisions. That's the definition of a lil' girl. And to be honest,

as much as I'm crazy about you, I ain't with that shit."
I blew air through my teeth and shook my head again.
"Your breakfast is on your dresser. I hope you enjoy
it." I turned my back on her and got ready to walk out
of the room.

She jumped out of the bed so fast that she
dropped the sheet to the carpet. Then, she was
grabbing my arm and pulling me back. "Jayden,
please, don't leave me right now. I need you. I want
to be your woman. I don't care what Nico says." She
blinked, and tears ran down her cheeks, looking into
my eyes with a pleading expression written across
her face.

I pulled my arm away from her. "Whitney, I
ain't got time for this shit, lil' mama. I got too much
on my plate to be playing games. So, what you need
to do is to take a few days to get your mind right, and
when you're ready to be with me wholeheartedly,
then I'll be there waiting for you with arms wide
open. Until then, I gotta go make a way for this
family. Nah' mean?" I turned the knob on the door
and started to pull it open.

She rushed over and slammed it so hard that it
sounded like a gunshot. She looked up at me with
anger on her face and tears streaming down her
cheeks. "Now you listen to me, Jayden. I am telling
you that I don't care what Nico thinks. I want you to
be my man, and that's what I'm going to get. I will do
anything that you want me to do to prove myself. All
you have to do is to tell me what you want. I just can't
be without your love right now. I need you; can't you
understand that?" She whimpered.

I sighed and pulled her into my embrace. I got to feeling bad and didn't want to play with her emotions like that. I knew that she needed me. I mean, she'd just lost her man and her brother all in the same month. I was the only source of normalcy in her life at that time with the exception of Janet, so I had to hold her down and give her the love and affection that she needed. Only a monster would have denied her that. I felt her crying against my chest.

"Shh, shh, it's okay, baby. I got you, and I love you, Whitney. If it's gon' be me and you, then let's do this. Let's take this one day at a time until we can get it down pact, okay?"

She nodded against my chest. "I just want you to love me, Jayden. It's all I ask. I don't care what you do in those streets. Just come home and love me. It's all I ask. Please."

Chapter 8

I lit the last Airwick candle and set it right next to the air conditioner that I'd brought for the trap that me and Naz served our dope out of. It was two days after me and Whitney had got an understanding amongst ourselves. I'd been sitting in the trap for the last four hours, popping heroin and talking things over with Naz. Earlier that day, Jazz had hit my phone saying that she was ready for me to pull the first caper. It was to take place that night, and I honestly couldn't wait. She assured me the we'd have eighty gees minimum to split between the two of us. That would be forty bands to the good. I'd give Naz five and he'd be cool with that, I was sure.

Naz slapped a clip inside of his Forty-Five and cocked it back. "Yo, I used to have this Rican bitch back in New York that would set up niggas for me. We fucked around for two years until one of the niggas that we were going to hit wound up blowing her head off with a sawed-off shotgun." He shook his head. "The most money I ever saw was when I was fucking with her. Shit, I really ain't no trap nigga, Jayden. I like taking money from niggas after they worked hard for it. All this sitting around and waiting for money to come is too slow for me, which is why this new shit you talking is right up my alley. How much you say I stand to make?" He asked, taking a cigarette from behind his ear and lighting the tip. He inhaled the gray smoke deeply and blew it out, sitting down on the funky couch that I was going to get rid of.

"You got a guaranteed five gees coming, even though I don't know the exact number we're supposed to get yet. I just know it's gon' be enough to hit you with at least five bands."

He nodded. "Yo, well if that's the case, you might as well just give me mine in dog food. I'll take five gees worth of heroin right now, and I'll pop that shit later. That way you can keep the money. That sound cool to you?" He pulled on his nose and sniffed hard, fidgeting on the couch and looking uncomfortable.

I exhaled slowly, a little irritated because it seemed like Naz's heroin habit was getting worst. I noticed that he was up to snorting about ten grams a day. It was probably more, but it was all I could confirm from watching him when he was in my presence. "Kid, what ever happened to the bread from the lick you hit the other day? You know, that vic outside of the cheese steak joint?" I asked trying not to frown too much.

He wiped his nose and swallowed. "Yo, I handled some bills and shit, and a few other obligations. Far as the dope, I still got that, and I don't know what I'ma do with it yet." He frowned. "It's cocaine. I don't fuck with that shit."

I walked over to the couch and sat on the edge of it before popping back up. I didn't wanna smell like that muhfucka at all. "How much cocaine is it?" I asked, digging into my crotch and pulling out my Ziploc bag of heroin. I opened the bag and counted the individual wrapped packages as fast as I could.

"It's eighteen zips, all powder. Why? You interested?" he asked, licking his lips, then pulled from his cigarette again.

I sat the Ziploc bag of dope down in front of him. "Here. That's you right there. It's like fifty-five hunnit worth, but its good. And, yeah, I want that dope too, especially if you ain't fucking with it. I'll give you five ounces of heroin for it, pure dog food, and you can step on that shit anyway you want to. How does that sound?" I asked taking a step closer to the air conditioner. I caught a whiff of my cousin's body odor and that shit almost made me sick. I hated the smell of a funky man worse than that of a woman any day. He must've not taken a shower in a few days or something, but I neglected to ask.

He peeled open one of the foiled packs and dumped it on the table, separating the contents before tooting them up one nostril at a time. Then, he sat back on the couch and lowered his eyes. "That White yours, lil' cuz. I ain't gon' do shit with it. I'll give it to you when we go back to my crib. I just need to party for a minute." He began dumping another pack out before doing his thing.

* * *

Five hours later, I was easing into the hotel room that Jazz had left slightly ajar, with a .9-millimeter in my hand while Naz followed close behind with a Forty-Five in his. The air inside the hotel room felt cool as if the air conditioner had been turned on full blast. There was also the scent of apple in the atmosphere. I ducked as low as my knees would allow me to as I eased through the door, going further into the room.

The further I got inside, the clearer the groans of a man became, until I was able to look ahead and see a tall, light skinned man with one of his feet on the bed, while Jazz was on her knees, with her eyes closed, giving him the head of his life. The audio of her slurping got louder and louder as I made my way toward them. The light skinned man had his head tilted backward with his eyes squeezed tight, fucking into her mouth. He was naked with nothing but his socks on.

I prepared myself for the attack, when all the sudden, Naz shot past me and ran toward them, slapping the dude with his Forty-Five so hard that he flew against the wall, and landed on top of the lamp. Both fell onto the floor with the man groaning.

"Shut the fuck up!" Naz slurred, grabbing the man by his shirt and dragging him across the floor before straddling him, placing his gun into his mouth. "Where is the money?"

Jazz let out a low scream and fell to the floor, covering her head. "Please don't kill me. I'm just a stripper," she whined.

I grabbed her by the hair and placed my face against her ear. "Bitch, shut the fuck up before I kill you. Now somebody better tell me where the money is. Let's go. I know it's here," I said through clenched teeth.

I stood up and pulled her along with me. She hit at my hands and made it look as if she were struggling against me.

Naz stuffed the barrel so far down the yellow man's throat that he began to gag. "Where is the money? I ain't gon' ask you again."

The man tried to say something, but it came out gargled because of the gun stuck down his throat. He kicked his legs wildly and closed his eyes, until finally Naz removed the gun. "It's in the trunk of my car, man. You can have it. Just let me go." He said with blood oozing out of the slit in his busted lips. He winced in pain as Naz put his forearm in his neck and applied pressure.

"Who is this bitch to you? Huh?"

He shook his head. "Just some whore from Oasis, man. I don't know her like that. We fuck every now and then, and that's all there is to it. If it's about her man, I swear I don't know nothing about this bitch," he said in a panic.

Naz shook his head. "N'all, I don't believe you. Cuz, take this bitch in the bathroom and blow her brains out. Let's see if this nigga really cares about her or not."

Jazz whimpered. "Nooo, he's telling the truth. I don't really know him. All we do is fuck here and there. Please, don't kill me. I don't have any money." She turned and looked down at the yellow man. "You better tell them where the money is, because I didn't even know you had any. Please, don't let them kill me."

Naz pressed the barrel of his gun to the yellow nigga's forehead. "What's it gone be, son? You gone tell me where that bread at fa real, or you gon' keep playing?" He slurred.

I didn't know what he was talking about. The yellow nigga had already said it was in trunk of his car. What more was there to hear? I threw Jazz on the floor beside them. "Hold this bitch. Nigga, where your pants at?" I asked, looking around until I located them all on my own. I picked them up, searching through them until I found the car keys. "Bitch, what kind of car do this nigga have, and where did y'all park?"

Jazz winced in pain as Naz situated her so that she was lying next to the yellow nigga. "It's the red Bentley that's parked outside. It'll be next to my black Lexus, about four rows back from the back door." She said before Naz forced her face into the carpet. He was handling her real rough.

"Look, man, you can have the money. You and your homeboy can take the money and my car, and just leave. I got insurance and that lil' bread ain't gon' hurt me none." He said, turning his face to the side so his words could reach me.

With that information, I hit it out of the hotel room after adjusting my ski mask.

* * *

Two hours later, after snatching the bag of money out of the trunk of the car, I met up with Jazz at her condo on the east side of Philly. I watched her pace, holding an ice pack to the back of her neck while I sat at her living room table counting the money.

"Jayden, I ain't fucking with yo' cousin no more. That nigga way too rough with me. He ain't have to do me like that." She continued to pace, moving the ice pack all around her neck. Before she'd placed it on there, I saw that it was a little purple from Naz's rough handling of her. But I still felt like she was being a little dramatic.

I licked my thumb and kept on counting. "He had to make that shit look as real as possible. The last thing you need is for homeboy to come back and get at you. I guarantee he won't be doing that now." I said, sliding her forty-five gees across the table toward her. "Here. This you right there. It's forty-five bands on the head. He had ninety even." I stuffed my portion inside of a Gucci knap sack. and zipped it back up."

Jazz came over and looked over the pile of money, flicking through the bills. "He still ain't have to do me like that. Besides, I ain't worried about Cortez. He acts all tough and shit, but he ain't really about that life like he claims to be. That nigga family got money. He shouldn't even be in the streets, but some people just gotta be down. To be honest, I'm more worried about this move with Buns. When is your cousin supposed to be handling him? Did he say?" She asked, picking up her stacks of money and walking across the carpet on bare feet. She stopped in the short hallway and turned around to look at me.

I stood up and sat my knap sack on the table. "I know how my mans get down. He'll handle that business when it's most convenient, so just chill and know that it's being taken care of. If you want, you can hit me with that fifty right now 'cuz Buns is as good as dead." I picked up the glass of water that she'd given me when I first got inside of her condo and took a swallow from it.

She shook her head. "Yeah, I think I'ma just wait until I get the news. I'm his emergency contact, so if anything happens to him, they gon' let me know what's good, ASAP. Once they reach out to me, I'll drop that money, but not until then. It ain't sweet, Jayden." She rolled her eyes and disappeared to the back of the house with her cash. I heard the bedroom door close.

She didn't return until five minutes later. She was smoking on a blunt and shaking something in her right hand.

"I got this blunt of Kush and a few Oxy's. You wanna roll a lil' bit with me?" She asked smiling. "I mean, we do have something to celebrate. Ninety gees in cash don't happen every day."

I walked into her living room and sat on the couch. "Bring that bud over here and sit yo' thick ass on my lap."

She bucked her eyes and then lowered them into slits, taking a few steps forward. "I don't like you talking to me like that. You sound like them pervert ass niggas from the club. Now I thought you was more of a boss than them." She mugged me with hatred, standing in front of me and looking into my eyes.

I dusted my lap off and tried to remain calm. I had to keep in mind that I needed her, plus I wasn't trying to be disrespectful no way. I called myself flirting with her more than anything. "My bad, Jazz, I ain't mean it like that. I was just fucking with you. Quit being all mean and shit and come over here and sit by me, since the lap is off limits." I patted the spot directly on the side of me.

She rolled her eyes and leaned down to push my knees together before sitting on my lap. "I ain't say the lap was off limits because I'm feeling you. I just don't want you coming at me all bogus and shit. I want my respect. Is that a problem?"

I wrapped my arm around her waist and pulled her back so that her back was up against my chest. "Nah, it ain't. But why don't you go ahead and spark that blunt. Let's ease our minds a little bit."

She placed my hand on her thigh and squeezed it just to feel its thickness. She was most definitely stacked. The Daisy Dukes she wore did very little to hide that fact. She put the blunt into my mouth and lit the tip. "This that good shit too. I got it from one of my plugs out in DC. This that same shit Barack was blowing when he was in the White House." She took two of the pills in her hand and swallowed them without a drop of water, then tried to hand me the final two. "Here. They go hand in hand."

I took the two white pills and popped them into my mouth, swallowing just like she had. I didn't even stop to think about what I was doing. I just did it.

"Yeah, you gon' like them. You ain't never did Oxy's before?" She asked, turning around to look at me. Her ass fell all the way into my lap and put some pressure on my pipe. It felt good.

I shook my head and took three puffs from the blunt. "N'all, but ever body I know has. They toot they shit though. I ain't never heard about nobody popping 'em." I inhaled the smoke deep into my lungs and closed my eyes for a few seconds. I took in the harsh feel and fell in love with how fast the high came.

She took the blunt out of my fingers and turned back around, laying her back to my chest. "I got so many vicks lined up for you, Jayden. If you keep fucking with me, I'll have you eating the way you're supposed to be eating in no time. A nigga like you supposed to be whipping a Bentley all through Philly just like that lame nigga is. I want you to have some real bands put up, not no one or two hundred thousand. That's chump change. Nigga, you gotta be a boss." She slowly moved her ass back and forth in my lap.

I don't even know if she knew she was doing it. I think it was just her natural instincts. I held her waist and rubbed all over her thick thighs. "I like hearing that shit you kicking, but you gotta stand on that. I'm 'bout whatever you 'bout. You tell me what's good and I'ma knock it off, ASAP. I gotta have that paper by every means."

She took a strong pull from the blunt, picked up the remote from the glass table and turned on the television. "This next lick you hit gotta be Buns' baby mother. We could get a hundred bands a piece. I mean, I know it's more than that, but it's at least that. Then, if we snatch the kid, Buns' niggas will put up a cool million for him. I know that for a fact. We'd get that shit in cash and be done with it. Shit, we could even leave Philly behind and get on some other shit— hit up some of them southern states where them niggas are a lil' slower than us. I got people in North Carolina. I've been down there more than a few times. Them niggas down there getting money, and a lot of it. It'll be so easy to part them from it, too. I got so many plans in my head, all I need is the right man's loyalty, and I swear I'll make us rich." She handed the blunt behind her for me to grab. "Holy shit."

She stood up and walked closer to the big television that hung on her wall, turning it all the way up as they reported a killing at the same prison that Buns and Nico were at. An inmate had been stabbed multiple times in the throat at the prison while showering. He'd been left for dead and was discovered by a correctional officer. They were not releasing the inmate's name at that time, and the prison had been placed on lockdown.

Jazz turned around to face me with a smile. "Do you think it's him? Huh? Would Nico go for his throat like they're saying?" she asked, and I could sense the excitement in her voice.

I shrugged. "Like I said, all you gotta do is be cool, and shit will be handled the way it's supposed to be."

As if on cue, her house phone rang, causing her to nearly jump out of her skin. She pressed mute on the television, and then answered it, taking a deep breath and placing a finger to her lips to tell me to hush as if I needed her to.

I nodded and took a deep pull from the blunt as my whole body went numb, and I started to feel incredibly high. So high I had to sit down. I could literally feel my blood coursing through my body, and my head felt as if it was being pulled backward. I smiled and took another pull from the blunt.

"Yes, this is her," she said into the phone, walking back and forth. "May I ask you what this is about?" More pacing, now she was chewing on one of her French manicured nails. "Today? Oh my god!"

she hollered. "No, no, no, please don't tell me that! Not Bundy! Not my husband!" she screamed into the phone before dropping it to the floor. She fell to her knees and glanced over at me with a big smile over her face, mouthing the words, "Buns is dead." Then, she sobbed loudly, picking the phone back up, placing it to her right ear. She sniffed loudly and whimpered, "Yes. Yes. I'll be out there right away. Thank you for calling me. I'll see you soon."

She hung up the phone and stood up. "Well, that bitch nigga's dead. Let me get this cash for you, and we can be on to the next one. We settled on fifty gees, right?" She popped back on her legs, causing her Daisy Dukes to rise into crease.

I nodded and puffed on the blunt. "Yeah, that's about right."

Chapter 9

Nico walked up to me and gave me a half-hug before I sat across from him in the small visiting room. He'd managed to grow a lil' beard, and in my opinion, it made him look like an old ass man. He sucked hiss teeth then picked up the Grape Soda Pop from the table and took a sip. It was three weeks after Buns' hit, and their prison was just getting off lockdown. As soon as Nico reached out and hit my phone, I jumped on the highway with Jane, so we could rollout to see him.

"Look, bruh, yo' moms gon' be in here in thirty minutes. I told her to give me a half hour with you before she strolled in, and she was cool with that. But we're on the clock. Anyway, I copped you a lawyer by the name of Daniel Kondos. He's a monster and one of the best defense attorneys in the state. His retainer was forty gees; that's paid. I put the other ten on your books, so you should be getting a receipt for that money later today." I said, grabbing the Sunkist orange pop from the table and taking a sip. Just like before, the visiting room was as hot as a desert, so I'd dressed in the lightest clothing that I could find, and I was still roasting.

Nico curled his upper lip. "I see this lil' bitch you fucking with handled business right away, huh?" He took a swallow from the soda before setting it on the table and leaning forward. "That bitch came off fifty gees like that, she gotta have some more paper put up. Why not hit her for all that shit and get me up out of here? That forty gees ain't gon' go that far. Once Daniel look over my case and prepare just a few hours of the paperwork, he'll need another deposit, so we gotta get a move on. Nah'mean?" He pinched his nose and sniffed loudly.

I frowned and lowered my eyes, looking him over closely. "Nigga, I just told you that I got you a lawyer, one of the best in the state, and that's your response?" I felt offended as hell.

He nodded. "Yeah, what was you expecting it to be?" He mugged me with anger building, looking into my eyes with his lowered.

I laughed and rolled my head around on my neck. "Kid, you acting real cocky right now. I ain't feeling this. You know I'm all for hitting licks and making sure we're good at all times, but it's like you don't appreciate shit. All you want me to do is to follow your every command, like I don't got shit under control or something. You see she coughed up that dough and held up her end, and the first thing you do is want to strip her like a nigga? Really?"

Nico sat on the edge of his chair. "Nigga, I don't give a fuck about that bitch! Fuck her! And you muthafucking right; if I smell cash I'ma have you go and get that shit because I'm in this muhfucka for you and me. Never forget that. You acting all brand new and shit. What happened to yo' cold heart? That bitch turning you into a bitch or something?" He hollered, getting ready to stand up.

Before he could quite get there, one of the guards came over and asked us if we could be a little quieter. That we were disturbing the other visitors. I still had my head lowered with rage coursing through me, so I didn't acknowledge his presence.

Nico scrunched his face and nodded. "Yeah, aight, we heard you, now keep it moving." He sat back in his chair and ran his hands all over his face as the guard turned his back to us and walked off. Then, he exhaled loudly and sat back on the edge of his chair, looking me over for a long time in silence. He sucked his teeth. "Fuck wrong with you?"

I trailed my eyes up and looked into his face, and as soon as we made eye contact, I felt my temper getting hot, so I had to look off, laughing to myself to keep calm. "Yo, I don't know what the fuck you got going on in here, Nico, but you better get yo' shit together before you fuck up a good thing. If you insinuate that I'm a bitch again, my nigga, I promise you, we gon' have a problem. I mean that with the upmost respect."

Nico leaned all the way forward and placed his hands on the table, sucking his teeth loudly, running his tongue back and forth across them. "Jayden, who the fuck you think you talking too, nigga, huh? You think because I'm in this bitch that you running shit now? You think it's sweet or something? Huh?" He asked fidgeting around with sweat pouring down the side of his face. He wiped it away and continued to mug me.

I was so heated that my vision was going hazy. I started to see red and my heart was pounding in my chest. I looked into his eyes and curled my upper lip. "Nigga, I'm talking to you and I don't give a fuck how you feel about it. It ain't got shit to do with where you are, or if you're sweet, or none of that shit. The fact of the matter is that you gon' respect me and honor my gangsta. Fall yo' ass in line and let me do what I gotta do to get yo' ass up out of here. That's it. Without me, there is no freedom. Get that?" I asked, balling my hands into fists. I was seconds away from leaping out of that seat and being all over his black ass.

Me and Nico had boxed over twenty times in our lives; both blessed with horrible tempers and pride issues. Out of the twenty fights, I'd say I was up about two or three though he was no pushover when it came to hand to hand combat. But as long as I fired first, he didn't stand a chance because I hit hard and swung fast.

He mugged me with hatred. "That's how you feel, Jayden?" he asked, moving around uncomfortably in his chair as if he were ready to shoot out of it, just as I was.

"Hell yeah, nigga. That's exactly how I feel. So now what?"

We looked over each other for a long time in silence, both mugging and giving off body languages that spoke hate. I was 'bout whatever he was. If he wanted to tear that visiting room up, then I was all for it. I ain't like feeling like another nigga was pimping me or something. There I was telling this nigga the good news and he made it seem like it wasn't enough, that I should have been doing more. He was ready to blow up my entire program for his own selfish reasons. Not once did he ask me if I was good, and that got to me.

Just then, the double doors opened to the visiting room and Janet came through them, holding her visitor's pass. She took it up to the visiting room sergeant and handed it to him before slowly making her way over to us.

Nico's face softened, then he swallowed. "Look, Jayden, we'll holler about this shit later. Don't let my moms see us at odds with each other. That'll crumble her. So, act like its good, but we definitely got some shit to squash." He grunted and stood up, waiting for her to make her way to him.

I stood up before she could make it there and picked up my pop from the table. "Nigga, I'ma get you out of here because I owe you that. But after you touch down, nigga, we gon' holler on some real shit, and you know what I mean." I walked away from the table, stopping beside Janet as she made her way in his direction. "Look, I ain't feeling well. I'll meet you back in the car. Enjoy your visit, mama, okay?" I kissed her on the cheek and looked over my shoulder at Nico.

He had a mug on his face that told me that he was having thoughts of killing me. I'd seen that same look on his face so many times before, whenever we were retaliating on an enemy, or going to war in general within the slums of Philly.

Janet smiled. "Okay, baby, I'll try. I hope you feel better. Mama will be out there in a few hours."

* * *

Two and half hours later, Janet came out to the car with a big smile on her face, and her yellow sundress blowing in the wind. I opened the passenger's door for her and waited for her to get in.

She got inside and closed it behind her. "Whew, I'm so glad to be out of there. It was burning up. Did Nico look a lil' skinny to you, baby?" She asked getting ready to pull her seatbelt around her. She turned one of the small vents in my car so that the air conditioner blew directly on her.

I nodded. "Yeah, he probably ain't eating that food in there. But he got plenty money on his books, so he really don't have to. But, anyway, I need you, mama. Right here, before I even pullout of this parking spot." I said as I watched a family of Puerto Ricans pull up beside my car and exit theirs before going inside of the prison.

Janet squeezed her thick thighs together. The way the air conditioner was blowing on her, it was causing her dress to flutter, exposing her brown skin. "What are you talking about, baby?" She took a tuft of her curly hair and placed it behind her left ear.

I leaned over and rubbed her thick thighs, trailing my hand into her center, then pulling her left leg open so I could feel all over her pussy-packed panties, only to discover that she wasn't wearing any. "I want some of this." I spread her thick lip and ran my fingers up and down and in between her crease, feeling her become wetter by the second. "I'm startin' to get jealous from having to share you with Nico. I know that sound crazy, but you're my mama too. Am I right?" I slid two fingers deep into her pussy and worked them in and out while she placed her right foot on the dashboard and leaned her head back.

"Unnn-a! Baby! Yes, you're my baby too, and I love you just as much. Uhh-a, shit, Jayden. Finger mommy." She opened her eyes and looked between her legs to see what I was doing. It was like the more

116

she watched, the wetter she became until there was juice pouring out of her like crazy.

"You want yo' baby, mama. You want some of me? Huh? You wanna fuck me right here in this parking lot? Tell me. You already ain't got no panties on. Was you trying to show Nico that pussy?" I sped up my fingering, going as deep as I could while she jerked in the seat.

"Uhhh! Jayden. Don't say that. It's dirty!" she moaned and humped into my attacking fingers. Her shoulder strap fell, exposing most of her supple breast.

I pushed my seat back. "Get up here and ride me, mama. Ride me like I know you wanna ride Nico. That's why you wore this short ass dress. Ain't it?"

In response, she rushed to climb over my lap. Once there, she reached under her and placed my dick head on her opening before humping into it. "Uh, uh, uh, uh, talk to me, Jayden. Talk that shit to me, please. Uhhh!" She rode me faster and faster while I held her ass.

I sucked on her neck and bit into it hard. "You're my mama now. This my pussy. You gon' fuck yo' baby every day if I want you to." I growled in her ear through short breaths.

She bounced harder. "You're. My. Baby. I'm. Yo'. Mama. Uh-shit! I'm yo' mama, Jayden." She kissed all over my lips, and fucked me as hard as she could, while I squeezed her big titties and pulled on the nipples.

In my head, I was Nico, fuckin' her thick ass, enjoying that forbidden pussy. The sundress that she wore was so short that I knew for a fact that she'd flashed him more than once during that two-and-a-half-hour visit. It was impossible not to. Just the thought of that made me wonder if she knew what she was doing and if she got some sort of excitement from it, and I got my answer real quick.

I grabbed her big ass with both hands, forcing her all the way up and slamming her down hard. "Fuck me like I'm Nico, mama. Ride me like I'm him, 'cause he wanna fuck you, too." I hissed into her ear.

That seemed to drive her crazy. She got to bouncing like she was riding a horse, sucking all over my neck and moaning in my ear. "Don't say that. Uhhh, please! Jayden, stop!"

"I'm Nico! You fucking Nico. Tell me you love this dick, mama."

She licked my neck and rode me faster. "I love it, Nico! Mama love it, Nico! Uhhh! I'm cuming! I'm cuming, Nico! Uhhhh-a!" She screamed, fucking me so hard that the car was moving back and forth like crazy.

The windows were already fogged up and the scent of her pussy was heavy on the inside. The pussy was sucking at me, gripping me in ways that only a vet could, and I loved it.

I sucked her left nipple into my mouth and came deep within her womb while she popped her ass and slammed her stomach into my own.

After we came, she stayed on top of me for another five minutes, breathing hard into my face, kissing my cheek and lips. "You do something to me, Jayden. All that shit you was saying to me drove me crazy, and I don't know why. Please don't tell Nico.

That would freak him out. I feel so weird." she said climbing off of me, then leaning over in the passenger's seat to suck her juices off my dick.

I started the car and pulled off, jumping on to the highway while she slobbered on my pole all the way home. She seemed as if she couldn't get enough of it. I came a block away from her house, humping into her mouth as she swallowed every drop of me; pumping my pipe, squeezing it within her fist until I was drained.

When I pulled in front of the house, I threw the car in park and started to fix my pants, buckling my Gucci belt and looking over at her. She had one of these distant expressions on her face as if she was happy and in a faraway land.

I frowned. "What's good with you?" I sucked my fingers one at a time, tasting her on them.

She shook her head. "Nothing, I was just thinking about you, that's all. The fact that you drive both me and Whitney crazy is no mystery to me. Have y'all been fucking for long?" She asked, pulling her dress down just a tad so it could cover a little more of her thick, brown thighs.

I laughed. "N'all, just for a lil' while. Why? You sounding like you're jealous or something. You think she gon' take me away from you?" I teased, taking my keys out of the ignition.

She smirked and laughed. "Yeah, right. Boy, I can tell that you got mommy issues. You need me just like I need your fine ass, 'cause I guess you can see what kind of issues I got." She blushed and shook her head. "I'm so embarrassed to admit that too, but whatever. Anyway, Jayden, you gotta be cool with my daughter though because she is emotionally vulnerable. And when she falls in love, she tends to love super hard. So, if she falls for you and finds out how we got down, it's going to shatter her. I know this for a fact. Not only that, but you gotta watch how you handle her all around the board because she'll put up a brave front, when in reality she's weak. Do you understand what I'm getting at?" She asked placing her hand on my thigh and squeezing it.

I nodded. "Yeah, I do, and I'll try my best to not hurt her, but I ain't perfect; you should already know that. I ain't trying to take it there with her either, but at the same time, I am feeling her more than I probably should be."

Janet cuffed my pipe, squeezed it through my jeans and took her hand away. "I think it's because of what you and Nico did to Lincoln and his father. There may be some sort of guilt there on your behalf. That, and my daughter really is a good girl. She's loyal, down to earth, and she looks just like me. So that's a plus." She laughed to herself. "Look, I'm not trying to stop fucking with you on our level. That dick is good, and it's what I need, especially if you gon' be talking that taboo shit in my ear while you're hitting places in me that I've dreamed of being hit. All I'm asking is that you do your best to shield her heart, and keep mommy in mind. Okay, baby?" She pulled her dress back and exposed her naked pussy. "You can't tell me that this box ain't fire. I saw yo' eyes roll back a couple times." She kissed me on the cheek before getting out of my whip and slamming the door behind her.

I watched her walk up the stairs with the wind blowing the dress all over her big ass. More than once it exposed her born cheeks with the light stretch marks across them. I had to shake my head. Man, I loved that body, and the more I got to despising my right hand man, the more his mother's delights appealed to me. Hers and Whitney's.

Chapter 10

Whoom! Naz kicked in the front door of the duplex and moved to the side so I could run in with both of my Forty-Four Desert Eagles extended, cocked back and ready to buss anything moving. As I ran in, there were three Mexican dudes with green bandannas around their necks sitting at a table, counting a pile of cash with blunts in their mouths.

"Bitch ass niggas, don't nobody move! Get the fuck down right now!" I said running over to the couch and smacking the one closest to me across the face with my gun.

He fell to the floor, holding his jaw while the other two dropped beside him.

Two of Naz's lil' homies ran further into the house while he followed close behind, holding a Mach 11 with an extended clip. "Yo, snatch up that money, god, and we gon' handle these fuck niggas in here." He said, leaving the front room.

I stomped my Jordan on the back of the nigga's neck that I slapped with my pistol, putting my gun inside of my waistband, then digging into my crotch and pulling out a big black plastic Hefty bag, popping it out. "A, you, get the fuck up and bag this money, right now, and hurry the fuck up before I body you," I said, kicking one of them in the side that looked to be about nineteen years of age.

He jumped, took the bag out of my hand and began to stuff it with the money that was all over the table while I heard Naz in the background giving orders, along with the niggas that he'd brought along for the ride. I heard somebody screaming in pain and I figured my cousin was forcing them to tell him where their stashes were.

Jazz told us that they should've had more than ten kilos of cocaine in this trap. One of the dudes had been a connect for Buns, that she'd known a little more personal than Buns knew about. Now that Buns was out of the picture, Jazz thought it would be easy for us to knock off as many of his old connects as possible. But only the ones that she knew firsthand, if you get my drift.

The teenager stuffed the bag with money with a mug on his face. "You ain't gon' get away with this, Essay. We'll find you, Homes; trust me on that. Nobody fucks with the Mexican Posse and lives to tell about it." He said throwing the last bit of money into the bag, and throwing it at my foot like he had an attitude or something.

There was a high-pitched scream followed by a crash, and then I heard Naz shouting orders again. "Take me to the dope! This my last time telling you!" he hollered.

"I'll take you. I'll take you," came a female voice.

I swung the pistol and smacked the young nigga so hard that I knocked him out cold. He fell across the table, sleep, with his right leg twitching.

The one that I'd smacked previously with my pistol jumped up and ran to his aid. "Junior! Junior!" He looked back at me with his face scrunched.

I aimed my gun directly at him. "Fuck you gon' do, tough guy? Huh? Bitch, I'll put a bunch of holes on top of your head like a salt shaker. Lay yo' punk ass down. Fuck Junior!"

He held his hands in the air and slowly kneeled with his face scrunched.

I began to search them one at a time—uncovering their weapons and throwing them into the bag. I couldn't believe that they were strapped and didn't shoot at us as soon as Naz kicked in the door. Had it been me, I would have emptied my clip. I didn't give a fuck if it had been the police or not. After all of their weapons were recovered I made them lie down with their hands over their heads while I held them at gunpoint.

Naz and his men were still somewhere in the house trying to locate the stash spots. I took the time in between to go into the bag and take out about fifteen thousand, stuffing it into my briefs. Naz didn't have to know exactly how much I had. I had to make sure I was good above all.

Ten minutes later, and with my anxiety going through the roof, Naz appeared with his guys. They ran past me and out of the house with me in tow. I closed the door behind me, then we ran full speed down the street and to the getaway Caravan, where I got behind the wheel and stormed away from the curb.

* * *

Jazz came over and sat on my lap, sipping on a glass of red wine; swishing it around in her mouth before swallowing it. "So how much is there, baby?" She kissed my cheeks and ran her hand all over my chest while I finished up my count.

"It's two hundred and twenty-five gees right here, so we get seventy-five a piece." I said to her and Naz.

Before I'd met up with Jazz, I'd taken another ten gees out, so with the seventy five, I was getting away with a hunnit gees flat, which in my opinion was a good lick. I slid seventy-five bands across the table to Naz while I watched him take one of the kilos of cocaine, separate it in half, and drop it into a clear bag before taking his money, and sliding a bunch of dope across the table toward us.

"Here. It was eleven kilos of coke in there, so here is seven and a half birds for y'all to split."

Jazz shook her head. "I'm good. I just want the cash, so y'all can give me five a piece for this dope and I'm straight." She stood up and grabbed her money, looking from me to Naz.

He shook his head. "Nah, I don't fuck with that white shit. I don't even want this. If he wanna give you five for it he can, but I'm good." He stuffed his dope and money into a blue and red Spiderman book bag and stood up. "Yo, I'm out, kid. I'll fuck with you in the morning on that trapping shit I was telling you about. Like I said before, I got a few of the lil' homies that's gon' push that product for us. I'ma get 'em set up, and you just make sure you fuck with me first thing in the morning. Nah'mean?" He walked around the table, and I stood up and gave him a half of hug. "Peace, god."

"Peace, bruh. Be safe out there, and make sure you give some of that bread to the wifey." I joked.

He frowned. "I'd never trick off on no bitch, and shorty definitely ain't nothing but my baby mother. Don't get it twisted. In fact, I'm finna go lay up with somethin' Brazilian right now." He nodded and threw up the deuces.

Jazz closed the door behind him and locked it, shaking her head. "Damn, every time I'm around yo' cousin I feel so uneasy. That fool nuts, I hope you know that." She said walking back to the table and picking up her glass of wine, taking a short sip out of it. "So, what you gon' do with these birds? You gon' give me that ten gees for them, or am I going out and finding a buyer?" She asked, picking up her money and making her way toward the hallway that lead to her bedroom.

I counted off five gees and handed it to her. "That's five more bands right there. That's all you getting. I'ma take this dope and flip this shit. We only said that we would divide up the money. You never said you wanted a portion of the dope, so don't try that shit. Take this bread, go and put it up and then come fuck with me." I gave her the money and walked back to the table and sat down, bunching the dope and money together before getting up and grabbing my duffle bag and bringing it back into the living room where I filled it with our spoils for the day.

I knew I had to check in on my mother, to see where her bills were at and her overall health. I missed her, and it had been a minute since I'd checked in with her physically.

Jazz came back into the living room five minutes later with a smile on her face. She was holding a bottle of Hennessy with the top off. She took a sip and swallowed before wiping her mouth.

"You think you finna get away with all of that dope, and you're only going to give me five gees for it?" She took another swallow and smiled, laughing to herself.

I grunted and took the blunt out of the ashtray, setting fire to it. "I don't feel like arguing with you, Jazz. Why don't you tell me what's good with this lick involving Bun's baby mother? You think she still got all of that paper there? Huh?" I inhaled deeply and blew the smoke in her direction.

"Do you think that just because I'm a female that you can play me for a fool, or that I'm not as gangsta as you or something?" She walked over and sat the bottle of Hennessy on the table and wiped her mouth with the back of her hand, before looking me over closely.

"Jazz, gon' with that dumb shit. I don't think nothing, one way or the other. Our deal was for the money, not the dope. Now that we came up with these birds, all of the sudden you hollering you want cuts from them. That ain't how the game go." I said getting irritated.

I was already thinking of how I was going to have Naz's lil' niggas push my product for me. I would pay them the bare minimum so I could take half of the profit and buy a nice amount of heroin, so I could flip that and make more money. I had a lot of bills to pay, and besides that I wanted to start to get my shine on a lil' bit, which was why I wanted Jazz to give me the ins and outs on Bun's baby mother's stash spots. I wanted to hit her ass, take his kid, and move in on that million dollars that she was speaking about earlier.

"I'll tell you what. I'ma give you this lil' punk ass five gees back, and you can give me three kilos. That way, I'll holler at a few real niggas and I'll wind up selling them for at least ten a piece. That's thirty gees, six times what you gave me for it." She exhaled loudly. "Jayden, I'm about my muthafuckin money. I don't know how you can't see that. I ain't about to let nobody play me for my bread; no way, no how. Now it's cool that you're greedy and all, because I am too, but you got me fucked up, and you're looking like you're about to bite the hand that's feeding you and your crew. Is that the case?" She asked, taking the blunt out of my hand aggressively.

I grabbed it back and flared my nostrils. "Look, shorty, don't talk to me like I'm one of them suckas you been having me hit. This ain't that. I'll fuck yo' lil' ass up. Word is bond." I said with my chest heaving.

"Oh yeah? And what the fuck you think I'ma do? What? Sit back and let you whoop me?" She laughed and walked over to the couch where she reached up under the cushions and pulled out a .9-millimeter Beretta, cocking it back. "Nigga, I know you strapped. I know you a killa, and that you 'bout that life. But I don't give a fuck about none of that right now. You gon' either give me five more bands, my dope back, or we about to shoot this bitch up. Word is bond. I ain't got shit to lose, nigga, so what's it gon' be?" She flared her nostrils now and took two steps toward me.

I was so taken aback that all I could do was laugh because apart of me couldn't take her seriously. I'd never seen a female act like her before, and it was honestly turning me on more than anything. "Aw, so you gon' shoot me, huh? Over five gees?"

She shook her head. "N'all, nigga, I'ma shoot you over thirty bands, and the fact that it had to come to this over some petty ass figures. So, it's the principle more than anything. But either way, you gon' honor me, and see me as more than a female."

I blew air through my teeth as I looked her lil' fine ass over. Standing there in her tight Prada jeans, cut off belly shirt that broadcasted the pink diamond in her belly button, she was braless; both nipples were visible through her top. Her lips were glossy, shining bright from the MAC that she'd applied to them that day. And even though her face was screwed into a frown, it did little to take away from her beauty. This girl was bad on all levels, and hood. For me that was the perfect combination. I wanted to fuck her and shoot her at the same damn time.

I sat down, went into my duffle bag, and counted out $5,000 before zipping it up and handing the money over to her. She stood right there in my face and counted it bill for bill. Licking her thumb, and smiling with her pistol in front of her waist band. The handle was up against her stomach.

After confirming that it was the right amount, she nodded. "Well, there we go. Now, was that so fucking hard?" She asked, laughing out loud.

I couldn't do nothing but laugh as she disappeared once again to the back room and closed the door.

Five minutes later she appeared. "Alright, look, the best time to hit this nigga's baby mother is this Wednesday after Buns' funeral. She'll be in a state of distress, tired from hosting, and ready to go to sleep. The only thing we'll have to worry about is if there is going to be someone there to console her, and if so, who he is. I mean, I know that you and Naz are goons so it won't be that much of a problem, but we still have to be careful. And for the record, there should be way more than three hundred grand. I'm projecting almost four hundred, because before Buns got popped off, he made a few deals that I'm just finding out about, and I won't say how I know, just trust me on this." She held her fingers out for the blunt and I passed it to her. "You wanna chill with me for the night? Maybe watch a movie or something?" She asked, walking to the couch with her jeans cuffing that fat ass. Then, she sat down and crossed her thick thighs, running her tongue across her lips, smiling seductively at me.

I came into the living room and sat across from her, looking her over closely. "You projecting four hundred. How are we splitting it, and keep in mind that I gotta use a nice amount of Naz's niggas to make it happen, unless you're saying that the move should be easy enough for me and him to hit on our own. What you think?" I had to pick her brain for a minute.

Four hunnit gees was life changing money. I was hoping there was a way that I could hit the lick on my own, that way instead of cutting Naz in, I'd just give her two hunnit gees and keep the other two, adding it with the money I already had. Then, I'd be able to make some power moves in the slums.

Jazz stood up and walked around the table, moving my arm out of the way, and sitting on my lap, facing me. "If we wanted to, you and I could hit this bitch on our own. I got the security code to her house and everything. We could wait until the wee hours of the night and get at her like that. If somebody else is there, we'd just have to body their ass. No matter what, we have to leave with the kid though. That'll add to whatever profit we come up with." She curled her upper lip, puffed off of the blunt, and inhaled the smoke deeply before blowing it to the ceiling. "If you wanna fuck with Naz, that's good too. I mean, it'll work either way, but I'd prefer to come away with the most cash possible, and the kid." She sat the blunt into the ashtray, then placed her forehead against mine. "What you wanna do, baby?"

I looked into her eyes and held her in my lap by cuffing that fat ass. Her perfume wafted up my nose and made me feel some type of way. I liked her because, in my opinion, she was a true hood chick, about her paper, and always looking forward to the next lick. I felt like I could fuck with her for a long time, because ever since I had, my bands had been increasing at an alarming rate. For a hustler, that was everything.

I kissed her lips and sat backward while still holding her ass. "I want you to do a lil' more research. Just make sure that if you and I handle this business on our own that shit will go smoothly without any surprises. If we can, then I got this shit, and we'll split the money two ways, and snatch his son. Seems simple enough. But you gotta make sure that we're good. You feel me?" I squeezed that ass and sat up so I could kiss her lips.

I didn't give a fuck that she was a stripper or sold pussy on the side. This lil' broad had my nose open because she was about that hustle game that intrigued me, so I had to taste them lips.

"Um, I got you, daddy, don't you worry." She kissed me again. "I feel like we'd make a great team if you quit being so damn petty. You need to know that if I'm fucking with you, and you're my nigga, that I'm gon' keep you eating good. Shit, Buns had it made until he decided to play me for a fool for this bitch that we'll be hitting this week. But you live and you learn. Now that nigga pushing up daises when he could've been pushing a Bentley truck." She laughed. "Nigga's underestimate this pussy between my legs more than they should." She leaned forward and kissed my lips again.

She lifted her head. "Oh, shit, what time is it?" She asked, getting off of my lap, picking her phone up off of the table and looking at its face. "Holy shit, I gotta get ready. It's gon' be a bunch of promoters in the house from out of Atlanta. I gotta do my thing, and if I do, I'll be headlining a few of their major clubs down that way. That'll be some serious paper." She looked down on me with a sad look on her face. "I'm sorry, Jayden, can we do this another time?"

I nodded and pulled her to me, wrapping my arms around her lil' frame. "It's good. I got way too much shit on my mind anyway. We'll get together sooner or later. I'd prefer it to be after we hit this lick though. That way we have something to celebrate." I leaned down and kissed her lips.

She laughed after we broke apart. "Nigga, if I'm letting you hit this pussy without paying for it, that's a reason right there to celebrate. Trust me."

Chapter 11

When I got home that night, Whitney met me at the door, dressed in a red, short, silk robe, with a candle in her hand. I stepped into the house and closed the door behind me, kicking my Jordan's off and setting them on the side of the door where a few other shoes were. Then I looked down on her. "Baby, what's the matter?"

She shook her head, taking hold of my hand. "There is nothing wrong. I just want you to come with me. Oh, and I've missed you, baby." She stood on her tippy toes and kissed my lips, closing her eyes and turning her head to the side, before breaking our kiss and leading me through the dark house that was only illuminated by the candle that she held in her hand. It smelled like vanilla.

She led me to the dining room where she already had our plates made up. She pulled out my chair and ordered me to sit before going around the table and sitting across from me. I looked down at my plate and saw that she'd made us New York strip steaks with a baked potato and broccoli. In the middle of the table was a bottle of white wine.

She poured us two glasses, handing one across the table to me. "Here you go, baby." Through the flickering of the candles that decorated the table, I could see her pretty eyes zooming in on me.

I took the glass and sipped out of it. "What's all this about, Whitney?" I set the glass down and looked across the table at her, feeling confused.

She shrugged and exhaled. "I just really missed you, and I wanted to do something special. My mother is at work for the whole night, and we have the house to ourselves. I hope I'm not doing too much, and if I am, please let me know." She lowered her head and seemed to be getting a little sad.

For some reason that hurt my heart because I knew that she meant well. I shook my head. "The food looks good, baby, and I appreciate you for making the effort. It means a lot to me, and I love you for it, fa real." I reached across the table and took a hand hold of her hand, clasping my fingers inside of hers.

She smiled. "You're welcome, baby, and I appreciate you too. I know who's paying all of the bills around here, and I also know that you managed to get Nico a really good lawyer that isn't cheap. It seems like you're really placing our entire family on your back, and somebody needs to tell you how important you are, so let me be the first. I appreciate you for everything you do for our family. I love you, and I know that there is no man in this world like you." She blinked tears out of the blue. "I want to be a part of you so bad." She sniffled and wiped her tears away.

I scooted my chair back and went around the table, pulling her to her feet, wrapping her in my arms and holding her with my lips pressed to her forehead. "I love you too, baby, and I'd do anything for you with no hesitation. You're my shorty, and it's my job to make sure you're straight at all times. You understand what I'm saying, baby?" I tilted her chin up so she could look into my eyes to see my sincerity.

I really cared about this woman, because every time I looked into her pretty face, I saw her as being that little girl that I'd protected for nearly all of her life. I saw somebody that I'd grown to love and care about, even more than I did Nico. Whitney was pure to me. Innocent, a good girl, little Red Riding Hood, and I felt like a hungry wolf that had to keep from eating her alive. I wanted so badly to solely care about her, and be with just her, but it was so hard because of my lifestyle, and because I felt I'd wind up hurting her down the road, even though I didn't know how. But this night, I was weak over her. I felt emotions for her within me that I didn't even know that I had.

She nodded. "I do, and I love you so much, Jayden." She closed her eyes, and I picked her up so she could wrap her thick thighs around me. She kissed my lips and I sucked all over hers. Our tongues wrestled as we moaned into each other's mouths.

After I blew out the candles downstairs, I carried her upstairs to her bedroom and laid her on the bed, while Jhene Aiko sang out of the speakers.

She laid back and opened her legs wide, causing her night gown to rise. "Jayden, I wanna submit myself to you. I want to be everything that you need me to be and more. I wanna be your slave, just as long as you'll love me and keep me first in this life." She crawled to her knees and came across the bed, unbuckling my pants. "Can I serve you, daddy?" She asked this looking up into my eyes all sexy like.

I ran my fingers through her hair and grabbed a handful of it, leaning down and kissing her lips while she pulled my pants down and allowed for me to step out of them. "Nah, I wanna serve you tonight. You're my baby girl, and I think it's time you be honored as such."

I picked her up and tossed her back on the bed, causing one of the pillows to fall on the floor. She adjusted herself on her elbows, scooted all the way backward until her back was against the headboard, then opened her legs wide, showing off the way her red panties were all up in her fat pussy. The crotch band had a pussy lip on each side of it.

I picked up her left pretty foot, leaned down, and kissed one toe at a time. They were pedicured perfectly and had Louis Vuitton's logo all over them. There was nothing more sexy to me than a woman that kept her toes done. Seeing that made me want to do everything to her body. I sucked one toe into my mouth, then went along the foot until I'd done each one that way. Then I rubbed her foot up and down my stomach muscles, watching them go over the ripples, before looking her in the eyes.

She rubbed her pussy, spreading the lips, keeping the crotch band separating it. "You're so fine, Jayden. I love you so, so much, big bruh. I'm serious." She sucked her fingers into her mouth, before returning them to her pussy, sliding her fingers under the band now.

I picked up her other foot and did the same thing to it that I'd done to the first one, then sucked my way up her inner thigh, all the way until I got to her pussy. She spread her legs wider and I pulled the panties upward until her sex lips were fully bared on each side. I sucked the right one into my mouth loudly, sliding my hand under her ass, and pulling her closer to me.

"Uhhh, Jayden," she whispered, yanking her panties to the side to give me all of the access I needed. She even spread the lips for me. "Eat me, big bruh. Eat me again. I need you." She whimpered, opening her legs as far as she could, grabbing my head and forcing me into her center where I attacked it like an animal. She was already dripping wet.

Her juices were all over my nose and mouth, but I sucked on her clit, licked up and down her crease hungrily, and slid my fingers in and out of her tight cat at full speed while she humped into my face and forced me to eat her all the more.

"Un, un, un, aww, yes, un, eat me, un, eat me, Jayden, eat me, it, feel, so good-a! Uhhh-a!" She closed her thighs around my head while she rode my face, making it hard for me to breathe.

I nipped at her clit with my teeth before sucking on it like a nipple.

She jerked and threw her head backward, forcing my face into her. "Un, un-a, un-a, un-a, aw-shit, aw-shit, un-a, I'm cuming, bruh! I'm cuming all over your face. Uhhhh-a!" She opened her thighs wide, grabbed the back of my head and rode my face while her pussy squirted juices all over my cheeks and chin.

I kept on slurping, sucking and swallowing until she collapsed on the bed with her legs wide open, rubbing her twat. I took my face and rubbed it all over her center, coating myself with it before getting to my knees, walking across the bed on them, grabbing a handful of her hair. With my dick, I put the big head on her lips before she opened her mouth and sucked him inside of it with hunger.

"Suck this dick, Whitney. Yeah, eat that up, baby. Good girl. That's my baby." I said, rubbing all over that fat ass booty.

She'd come to all fours. I pulled one of her ass cheeks away from the other one, causing her crinkle to expose itself. I ran my finger all around it before slapping her on the ass hard, squeezing it. She was so fucking innocent.

She sucked me faster and faster, slobbering all over my pipe, licking around the head and running her fist up and down him at full speed while her lips kept the head trapped. "I want to taste you, Jayden. Please. I wanna taste you so bad." She said after popping my dick out of her mouth, and rubbing it all over her face and eye lids.

I pushed her away from me, onto her stomach, got behind her, spread her ass cheeks, and licked up and down her asshole before forcing my tongue deep within her ass, slobbering all over it on purpose. I could smell the aroma of her pussy from this angle. She was on fire, oozing her cream, thirsty to be penetrated.

"Uhh, you're licking me there, Jayden. Unnn! You so nasty, baby. You so fucking nasty." She reached back and spread her ass cheeks then planted her face into the bed while I ate her ass out.

I watched her pinch her clit, and scream at the top of her lungs. I licked, sucked, and twirled my tongue in a circle before getting to my knees and forcing her face into the bed.

Once there, I placed my dick head on her asshole, rubbing her pussy, coating my dick with her juices. "This my body, Whitney. I own this. You understand me?"

"Yes, daddy. I submit. Take me. Take me however you want me. I'm yours. Own me! Own me! Please!" She begged.

I slammed my dick into her ass, feeling the heat surround me immediately. It was a tight fit, and I felt suffocated in a good way.

She turned her head to the side to face me with it scrunched. "I'm yours, Jayden, now fuck me. Own me." She slammed back on me, taking all of my dick. "Uhhhh! Yes, yes, yes, yes, yes, uh, uh, uh, uhhh-a, yes, fuck me, fuck me, baby! Fuck meeeee-ah!" She got to slamming back into me so hard that I had to grab her hips to stay aboard.

Watching her ass jiggle and her fingers play between her legs became too much. I grabbed her hair and pulled her head backward before cuming deep within that tight asshole.

The next thing I knew, we were in the shower, with her bent overand me going full fledge into her pussy from the back while she hollered and screamed my name. She was telling me how much she loved me and never wanted me to leave her side. I came so many times in her that I lost count. We didn't call it a wrap for the night until I was unable to rise and she was too sore to do anything else. But by that time, we were both exhausted.

* * *

The next morning, I woke up to Whitney pushing me on the shoulder again and again. I opened my eyes, and for a few seconds she looked blurry and was out of focus. I was so tired that I couldn't think straight.

She tried to hand me the phone. "Here. It's Nico on the phone and he wanna talk to you."

I yawned and stretched my arms over my head, shaking my head to get some of the cob webs out of it before grabbing the phone and smacking Whitney on that big ol' ass, watching it ripple. "What's good, kid?" I asked sitting up against the headboard of Whitney's bed. I could still taste her pussy on my tongue. I smiled when I thought about that.

"Ain't no what's good, nigga." Nico snapped. "What the fuck this lawyer talking about he ain't gon' be able to get me up out of here for at least six months? I thought he was the best in the state?" He shouted into the phone.

I exhaled loudly. "I ain't say he was the best in the state, I said he was one of the best. He comes highly recommended, and if he saying that's the earliest, then that's what it is. What you want me to do about it?" I asked, getting irritated.

First of all, I hated arguing the first thing in the morning. It made me wanna kill somebody. Secondly, I ain't like how Nico was coming at me. I felt like a bitch or something.

"Fuck you mean what I want you to do? I want you to get me somebody better than him, and for you to stop playing with my freedom, bruh. Look, I don't know why you think it's so sweet because I'm in this bitch. You know how I get down, nigga, and you constantly testing me. Had I known you was gon' be on this fuck shit I would've never did what I did. Word is bond." He exhaled into the phone. "I got this other lawyer by the name of Gerald Boyle. He say he can get me out of here in less than a month, but it's gon' cost us a hunnit and fifty gees. Now, I know you got it, bruh, so make that shit happen, fa real. I'm tired of playing with you."

I was gripping my phone so hard that I didn't even know it was slowly cracking until a piece of the top popped open. I was seething and I felt like I was about to blow a gasket. "Nico, nigga, you gon' have to chill out on the way you delivering this shit to me. You coming at me like I'm yo' bitch instead of yo' right hand man, nigga, and that's starting to piss me off. Now, I don't know why you keep on reminding me of how you get down, but let me also remind you of how I get it in too. Ain't shit sweet in this direction either, and you know that."

"What? Fuck you saying, nigga?" I heard a loud bang as if he'd punched something. "Nigga, until you get me up out of this muhfucka, you is my bitch! I thought you knew. I'm in this mufucka fa you and me, not just me. I could've let yo' punk ass take the fall for this bullshit, but n'all, I was more of a gangsta than that. Stuck to the G-code and this how you repay me. Dawg, if you don't come up with them chips and get 'em to this lawyer, on my mother's head, you gon' wish you would have. Now play with me if you want to. I done already gave my mother the information, so make that shit happen. You hear me?"

I crushed the phone in my hand and threw it to the floor, breaking it into a hundred pieces, then looking down at them with my chest heaving.

Whitney appeared in the doorway along with Janet. Whitney had one hand covering her mouth while Janet looked me up and down with a worried expression on her face. I was standing on the side of the bed in just my boxers. I was so mad that I could have shot the whole house up.

"Are you okay, baby?" Janet asking, squeezing through the doorway, walking over to me and placing her hand on my chest.

I flared my nostrils and took a deep breath. "I'm good. I'm alright. Just yo' son. Sometimes the homey can be too much to deal with. He acting like I ain't doing all that I can to get his ass up out of there. I just dropped fifty bands on his attorney, now he saying screw that one, and drop another hunnit for a different one that's possibly making him false promises. This driving me crazy." I sat on the bed and lowered my head.

Janet sat beside me, laying her head on my shoulder. "It's okay, son. We know that you're doing the best that you can, and it's not easy. I think that Nico is stressed out right now. Did he tell you that they came and questioned him about the other thing?" She asked, picking her head up from my shoulders and bucking her eyes when she said the last part.

Whitney came into the room and sat on the other side of me. "What other thing? He didn't say anything to me about anything, and we don't keep secrets from each other." She said, biting her fingernail.

Even though I was irritated, the scent of her still did something to me. I think I was falling for her for real. It had started out as me fucking with her because Nico had pissed me off, but now I felt emotionally attached to her, and for me that was crazy, because my heart was as cold as ice.

"Yeah, well, some things your brother has to keep from you just so you can't be a part of it, but I'm sure he'll tell you when the time is right. For now, it must not be."

Whitney frowned. "Then why would he tell you?"

Janet shrugged. "I don't know, but can we talk about this later. Clearly Jayden needs our comfort right now." She said, kissing me on the cheek and rubbing my chest.

I don't know what happened inside of Whitney, but all of the sudden she snapped. "Mama, I got this. If he need anybody to comfort him, I'll take care of that. I don't like how you're all over him. He's my man. Let me make that clear right now because I see how you look at him." She bounced off of the bed and walked to her bedroom door. "You can go, I got this."

Janet looked her over for a long time and laughed to herself. "Oh, so you're over Lincoln that quick, huh?" She shook her head. "Chile, I'll tell you, these kids today. Um, I just don't know what to do." She said, walking into the doorway after brushing past Whitney. She stopped and looked over her shoulder at me. "Son, if you need me, I'll be in my room whenever you need to be comforted." She looked Whitney up and down and shook her head again. "Be careful, Whitney, he ain't no Lincoln. That boy is a savage, and you already know what's

gon' happen when Nico finds out about you two."
She sighed and walked off.

Whitney waved her off. "I don't care what Nico
says. I love this man and this who I'ma be with. Nico
own you, he don't own me. Jayden owns me. Ain't
that right, baby?" She asked looking over to me.

I nodded and smiled weakly. My mind was on
the fact that them people had come to holler at Nico
in regards to Lincoln and his father's murder. I
wondered why he didn't find a way to tell me that
they had. He could have easily sent the message
through Janet, but the fact that he didn't had me a lil'
suspicious.

Whitney closed the door and walked over to
me, standing in between my legs. "Baby, is there
anything that I can do for you to make you feel
better? I'll do anything." She kneeled and looked up
at me with her pretty brown eyes.

I took her small face into my hands and rubbed
her cheek with my right thumb. "N'all, ma. All I ask
is that you don't switch up on me when Nico gets
home. I really do love you, and I wanna go hard for
you, if you'll allow me too, but I can already see that
you're going to have to choose either me or him."

She shrugged. "I choose you. It's a no brainer
for me. I been loving you ever since I was a little girl.
You've always been my protector, and you've loved
me even when I didn't understand it. You're my heart,
Jayden. I don't care that you're an animal, or that you
are Nico's best friend. I need to be with you to have
a purpose to live. I'm serious." She stood up and
hugged me.

I came off of the bed and wrapped her into my arms, holding her for a long time, kissing her forehead. I knew right then from there on out that I was going to do all that I could to go hard for her. I really cared about Whitney, and even though I knew that I was living on borrowed time, for as long as I was alive, I was going to do all that I could for her.

I kissed her forehead once again. "I love you, Whitney. I mean that with all of my heart. I gotta have you for myself. You have to belong to me. Ain't no other way around it, so I gotta get you away from here so it can just be us. Aiight?" I asked, looking into her eyes again.

She nodded. "Jayden, I'll do whatever you want me to do. I'll go wherever you want me to go, and all I ask is that you forever love me."

Chapter 12

"Okay, so we'll be able to hit that bitch tonight after the funeral. I found out that she did hire security to watch over her and her son, but it's one of the bouncers from the club who I'm real familiar with, so it ain't gon' be no thang. He acts tough, but he's actually softer than tissue paper." Jazz said walking across her carpet and handing me a plate of fried chicken, collard greens, and a big piece of Jiffy mix corn bread.

I shook up the bottle of hot sauce and got to pouring it everywhere. My stomach was growling, and the food smelt so good that I couldn't wait to bite into it. "So, you sure it's gon' be easy-breezy. This nigga ain't carrying no pistol or nothing like that?" I asked, twisting the cap back onto the hot sauce.

She pulled her chair out and sat down across from me, forking up a mouthful of greens. "Aw, I don't know, but I want you to kill him anyway. I never liked his bitch ass. He was always too touchy-feely for me when I first started at Oasis. Plus, I asked him too many questions that might not make sense to him now, but they will later. We can't take those chances. So, you gotta knock his head off and we gotta keep it moving. Oh, Buns' mother is going to be there too, just for a heads up."

I nodded. "I guess I'll be tying her ass up too. It is what it is, long as we get the money and the kid, right?" I bit into my chicken and closed my eyes, loving the sound and the feel of the loud crunch. Um-mmm, that girl could cook.

She peeled the skin off of her chicken and tossed it into her mouth, chewing loudly. "Yeah, no matter how much money we get, if we can get that lil' boy up out of them, we're looking at a million-dollar ransom that will be paid in cash. I been doing my research. Buns got a lot of people that owe him favors. Just because he's dead doesn't mean that his brother, Boonie, ain't still handling his business out in Jersey City. That nigga is large and I'm sure that before Buns got killed he let Boonie know what it was with whoever owed him this or that. Oh my god, I put my feet in this shit, didn't I?" She closed her eyes and smiled, shaking her head.

I swallowed the greens that were in my mouth and picked up the glass of Fruit Punch that she'd set before me, taking a nice, long swallow from it, quenching my thirst. "Aiight, Jazz, then I say we handle this business tomorrow, and get on with our lives. I'm trying to handle a bunch of shit right now, and I'd be lying if I said that I didn't feel weighed down to the max. Life is a bitch sometimes." I exhaled and started to fork up some of my greens before putting them into my mouth.

She smiled and looked across the table at me. "Nah, Jayden, you see, that's where you're wrong, because life is a bitch all the time, and everything that takes place in this world is because of a bitch, believe it or not. We make this muthafucka go 'round. I wish niggas understood that." She laughed and tore meat away from her chicken, then put it into her mouth.

* * *

Naz sat the Mach 11 on the table and pulled on his nose before sniffing loudly. "Aiight, Jayden, these my lil' niggas right here. That's Poppa right there, and this is Kilroy. These lil' niggas about that trapping life, and they come from a whole click of shooters that niggas in Philly have nightmares about. I want them to run under you, long as you putting food on their table, and clothes on their shorties' backs, these lil' niggas a buss their guns for you and keep your traps jumping like LeBron. I got a lot of love for these niggas, and I stand by their gangsta, nah'mean? Y'all gon' head and introduce yourselves. Got me talking for y'all and shit. This my cousin Jayden, and son wanna put you niggas on, fa real."

Kilroy, a dark skinned, heavy-set nigga with short dreads got up from the couch and nodded. "What it do, kid?" He walked over and gave me a half of hug. He smelled like weed smoke and alcohol. "I'm the head of the Shooters. Big homie saying you need some lil' young niggas to push a lot of product for you out here in Philly. Now, usually hearing some shit like that me and my niggas would take a good look at you, but seeing as your cousin is Naz, we come to you humble and ready to work." He lifted his shirt and exposed the fact that he had a waistband full of hand pistols. He looked into my eyes and smiled.

Poppa, a light skinned, musclebound built lil' nigga with long dreads and a mouth full of golds stood up and extended his hand, shaking mine. "What it do, kid? I'm Poppa. I get the name from my old man. He from the Bronx and got street respect just like me and my crew out here in Philly. We been pulling kick-doors for the last three summers. It's time for us to get put up on some real money that don't come with so much danger, if you getting my drift." He smiled and looked over his shoulder at Kilroy.

Kilroy laughed. "We ain't ducking no action though. Word is bond, these pistols is all I know." He sucked his teeth and lowered his shirt over his arsenal of weapons.

"Yeah, but that's why you niggas ain't got no money. Both of y'all peoples are starving because you're going about shit all wrong. But my cousin gon' really put you up on game. You niggas about to be eating fa real now. Tell me what's good, Jayden." Naz said sitting on the couch, taking a silver packet of heroin and dumping it on to the coffee table, preparing it to be snorted up his nose. He licked his index finger and ran it all around inside of both nostrils, then wiped that finger on his pants.

I reached into the duffle bag and came up with one of the kilos of cocaine that I'd gotten from the Spanish lick that Jazz had put us up on. I sat the kilo on the table and looked across it to Kilroy and Poppa. "Check this out. This thirty-six ounces of pure cocaine that I'ma cook up so we can keep this shit potent and give the feens the best quality of dope for their buck. We ain't fucking with weight. We gon' turn this into a dime Trap. Eight dimes for each gram, that's two thousand and forty dollars an ounce, and eighty thousand, six hundred and forty dollars for each key. No shorts. I'll pay both of you five gees a week, and for every two kilos that you serve for me, I'll give you a half of kilo for your crew. You'll get paid every Friday just like the rest of the world. Keep everything on the up and up and we'll eat together, nah'mean?"

Kilroy nodded and stood up. "That's what the fuck I'm talking about, son. Word is bond. We been looking for a real nigga like you. All we need is that chance to get on, and I swear we'll never look back. I appreciate you for looking out for the Shooters, kid. Word to my mother."

Poppa sat there rubbing his chin and nodding at the same time, as if he was lost in a deep thought.

"Poppa, you got somthin' on yo mind, kid? If so, speak up," I said, pushing my chair back from the table and looking him over closely.

"Aw, it ain't nothing. I was just thinking that if this dope is as pure as you say it is then I can whip this kilo for us and probably could make us about five hundred and sixty dollars more for each ounce. That'll bring our total for each kilo up to a hundred thousand and eight hundred dollars. I been whipping that work my whole life and I got some tricks up my sleeve."

"Will the dope still be as potent?" I asked, not willing to sell bunk ass dope just because the profits would be better. Even though I was in the slums, I tried my best to treat the feens as fairly as I could. I knew they'd kill you over that shit.

Poppa shook his head. "Oh, hell n'all, not the way I do it. Our dope will still be one hunnit, and the bags will be bigger than them fools over on the Avenue. They're our only competition right now." He said, curling his upper lip.

Kilroy stood up and took a gun from his waistband, cocking the Nine back. "I mean, we could go and shut that bitch down before we get started over here. That way we won't have to worry about no competition. I'm trying to make the most money that we possibly can. We got a bunch of Shooters from the Projects that are depending on us, Poppa, and they steady cutting all of our parents' government funding. I'm tired of seeing all of those single mothers in our Projects struggling to make ends meet. We got the hood on our backs."

"Which is why using them hammers right now ain't gon' do shit but slow our money all the way down. We gotta use our heads. Let's fuck with the homey, break this kilo down, I'ma chef that bitch and we'll go from there. If somewhere down the line them niggas on the Avenue are still a problem, then we'll take a good look at them. You feel me?" Poppa asked, looking at Kilroy from the side of his eye.

Kilroy curled his upper lip and placed his pistol back onto his waist. "Yeah, aiight. I guess I'll listen 'cause I said you was gon' be in charge of this hustle shit. But I'm letting you know now that I can't go that long without doing shit the old way. It's what I'm used to." He plopped down on the couch and took a blunt out of his shirt pocket, bussing it down the middle.

Poppa walked up to me and shook his head. "I thought we was gon' be moving that heroin for you too. I mean, the coke is cool, but this hood is mostly heroin addicts. What's good?"

I laughed and placed my hand on his shoulder. "First thing's first. Let's get this coke up and running and then we'll move on to the next drug. Gotta crawl before we walk. Get a feel for one another, nah'mean?"

He nodded. "Well, I'ma hit up the store and I'll be right back so I can chef that bitch to death. I'm telling you I'm a beast. Can't nobody fuck with my business when it comes to this shit." He took the two by four off of the door and handed it to me, unlocked it, stepped out, and closed it behind him. "I'll be right back."

As soon as he left, Kilroy jumped up from the couch and walked over to me with a crazy smile on his face. "Yo, can I talk to you back here for a minute, son?" he asked, nodding toward the back of the trap.

"Yeah, come on," I said, looking over at Naz as he leaned his head down and tooted up a thick line of heroin. It seemed that his lines were growing each time I saw him use.

When we got to the back of the trap, he ran his hand over his face and exhaled loudly. "Man, yo' name ringing through the streets of Philly, kid. It's a pleasure to finally meet you." He nodded and laughed. "I heard about Nico getting pinched and I'm sorry to hear that. I know that's yo' right hand man and all, but I ain't call you back here to say that. What I wanna know is where the action is. I know you got beef with plenty of niggas. Let me knock a few of 'em off for you so I can make some quick money. This hustling shit is more of Poppa's thing. I like to kill niggas and make they hoods write they names on the wall. I'll knock any nigga's head off for you at five bands a piece. I'm talking niggas, bitches, kids, old folks, it don't matter. Just give me the address and watch me work. I got a bunch of Project kids that's down just like me. I call them my family. We like fifty deep." He took his lighter and lit his blunt.

I rubbed the hairs on my chin and smiled. "You anxious to wet some shit, huh, lil' homie?" I liked what I was seeing, and I knew in time that I was going to be able to use him and his crew of hungry savages.

I was hoping that everything went right with Jazz, but if it didn't, it would be wise to have a crew of killas surrounding me, just in case I had to go to war with Buns' people. Not only that, I didn't know how things were going to fair with Nico. He seemed as if he had a lot of hostility in his heart, and I could only image what it would fester into, because I wasn't sure if I was going to drop a hunnit bands for another lawyer. That shit seemed pointless to me.

Kilroy pulled off of his blunt and blew a cloud of smoke to the ceiling. "I hate niggas, son. Word is bond, my heart is cold. I been through a lot, and all I know is these hammers."

I nodded, grabbed his hand and gave him a half-hug. "Aiight then, I'm gon' hire you on some solo shit. I'ma still pay you that five gees a week, but I'm also gon' pay you another ten, that way you can feed your crew. And whenever I need you and them to handle business, I'm coming to you. Deal?"

"Deal, kid. Word to my mother, you ain't never met a goon like me before. My loyalty is real." He hugged me again and patted me on the back with the blunt in his hand.

When Poppa got back, we sat in the kitchen for the next three hours cooking up the kilo of dope, while Naz sat on the couch getting higher than a kite. I watched him nod in and out and scratch blood out of his arm, before leaning forward and tooting some more. I felt sorry for him and Shawn, and decided that after I left the trap that night I was going to stop by his crib and drop off a few bands to her, just to make sure that she and my lil' cousin were straight. So, after me and Poppa finished whipping the brick, it's exactly what I did.

She answered the door with a short robe on and a toothbrush in her mouth. Her hair was pulled back into a pony tail, and she looked a little tired, as if it had been a few days since she'd gotten a good night's rest. I stepped into the house and closed the door behind me as she walked away from the door, her big booty jiggling underneath her robe.

"I take it Naz ain't coming home tonight, huh?" she asked, looking over her shoulder briefly.

I shook my head. "N'all, he said he gon' trap for the rest of this night to see how much he can come up with. You know how the homey is." I said coming into the living room, taking a deep breath and loving the scent of the incent that was sticking out of the wall.

She frowned and shook her head, disappeared into the back of the house and came back a minute later with a face towel in her hand, wiping her mouth. "I don't know what he doing with the money because we're behind on everything. Naz ain't paid a bill in this house since the second month that we moved in. I'm so tired of going through this shit, Jayden. I wished you would have never introduced me to him." She lowered her head, walked over to their sofa and sat down on it, looking at the floor. "I'm so close to giving up. I'm serious, I don't know how much more I can take of this. This is not what I envisioned for my future, Jayden." Tears fell out of her eyes and dripped onto the floor.

I took the seat right next to her and put my arm around her, pulling her to my chest, after wrapping my arm around her small shoulder. A part of me felt responsible for what she was going through because I had been the one to introduce them. I had sweet-talked her into going out with him more than once. Now that I saw what he'd become, it hurt my heart because there wasn't just the two of them, but there was also a child involved— my little cousin, Naz Jr.

"Shawn, I can't say for certain that I know what you're going through, but what I can say is that you're not alone. I'm here for you in any way that I can be." I held her tighter.

She broke into a fit of sobs, and started to shake badly. "He don't even care about me, Jayden. He ain't touched me since I told him that I was pregnant with his son. He acts like I disgust him when I should be the one turned off at all of the drugs I see him shove up his nose." She shook her head. "He hasn't even held our son for more than five minutes at a time. He's just a baby, it's not his fault. All he needs is his father's love." She rocked back and forth, continuing to break down.

I held her more firmly and closer to my heart. I hated hearing a female cry. It got the best of me. Shawn had always been a real good girl, and one hunnit on so many levels. I didn't understand why Naz treated her the way that he did, but it made me sick on the stomach. She started to shutter in my arms.

"Shawn, calm down. Listen to me. Everything is going to be okay. I got you. I'll fill in any blanks that you need me to, until my cousin gets his head back on straight, starting with your bills. Here." I broke our embrace, so I could dig in my pocket. I pulled out a knot of cash and counted off fifty one hundred dollar bills. "This five gees right here. This should help you to get caught up with your bills. Then take this right here and get whatever you and my lil' cousin need," I said counting off another five stacks and handing it to her.

She took the money and started to cry harder. "Why didn't you keep me, Jayden? It should have been me and you, and not Naz. I shouldn't have to depend on you to handle his responsibilities for him. He's a man, and as a man he's supposed to hold this family up, not down. I wish you would have seen the potential in me and never gave me away. I loved you so much back then. I still do." She faced me and wrapped her arms around my neck, lifting her head up so she could kiss my lips.

I allowed for her to suck all over them and swipe them with her tongue before I broke the embrace. "Shawn, this ain't gotta go down like that. I know you thinking that since I gave you that money that I expect something from you, but I don't. I just feel like I gotta have your back because I am the one that put you in this impossible situation." I rubbed her pretty face, then held it in my hand.

She grabbed my left hand and kissed its palm. "It ain't got nothin' to do with this money, Jayden. I never fell out of love with you. You have always been a major part of me, whether you knew it or not. Then, on top of that, I ain't been touched in so long. I'm in desperate need of some affection right now. I mean, I'll take whatever you can give me." She looked into my eyes, leaned forward and kissed my lips again before setting the money to the side of us and straddling my lap. Both thick thighs were on each side of me.

The first person that flashed into my mind was not Naz, it was Whitney. I felt like she was somewhere watching me while Shawn sucked all over my neck, and I held her panty-covered ass in my hands. "Shawn, chill, ma. Just let me hold you for a minute. That's what you need." I said as she bit into my neck and caused my dick to jump.

She stuck her tongue into my ear and twirled it around. "Forget holding me, Jayden, I need your body, if only a little bit of it." She took my hand and forced it between us. It wound up on her panty front.

I couldn't stop myself from feeling how fat it was. She was definitely packing. I couldn't believe Naz wasn't hitting that on a daily basis. I squeezed it between my fingers and pressed on its center, causing the panties to give her a wedgie.

"Mmm, yes, please keep touching me, Jayden. You ain't gotta fuck me, just keep on touching me, and telling me that you care about me. That you'll be here for me no matter what. Please, I need to hear that so bad. Fuck this." She stood up and slid her panties down her legs and straddled me again, directing my hand back between her legs.

As soon as my hand landed, I started to rub her pussy in short, fast circles, while my thumb played over her clitoris. I kissed her lips and breathed heavily into her mouth.

"Unn, mmm, yes, Jayden, yes, it feel so good. Faster, please, go faster," she moaned, humping into my hand, licking all over my lips.

I rubbed faster and harder, leaned my head to the side and sucked on her neck, and scraped the thick vein that ran alongside of it with my teeth, feeling my dick throbbing in my Gucci pants.

"Uhhh, mmmm-uh! Yes, yes, please, Jayden. I'm so sorry, I'm so sorry." She whimpered, throwing her head back.

I picked her up and sat her back on the couch, kneeled, and forced her thighs to her chest, bussing that pussy wide open before I sucked her sex lips into my mouth one at a time, licking up and down her crease, sucking on her erect clit, noting how big it was.

She bucked into my mouth, arched her back, and screamed. "Ahhh-Jayden! Oh shit!" She started to shake uncontrollably while I forced her knees further to her chest, and kept on sucking like crazy, loving the taste of her and knowing that I was healing her as best I could.

I stayed there on my knees and ate that pussy until she came five times in a row, then I picked her up and carried her into her bedroom, laid her beside my little cousin, kissed her on the forehead, and left her snoring right next to him. Even though I had crossed my cousin, I didn't give a fuck. In my opinion, I did what I had to make his woman keep her strength to keep on fighting forward.

Chapter 13

I slid the white ski mask down my face, then wiggled my fingers into the black gloves that covered them, took a deep breath, and opened my driver's door, grabbing the small bag of items that I'd need for the kidnapping that me and Jazz were about to pull off. I looked to my right and watched her pull her mask down before getting out of the passenger's side and closing the door slowly behind her.

She crept around the car and wound up on the side of me. "You sure we can leave this car in the alley and ain't nobody gon' do nothing to it? The worst case scenario would be to come back here and this bitch is gone. Where would we put the kid?" she asked, scratching her face through the mask.

I put my finger to my lips over the mask. "Shhh. First rule of hitting a lick, you don't speak negativity into existence. If that shit happens then we'll improvise, now come on." I sped down the alley at a slow enough pace so she could keep up with me. I was already starting to regret bringing her along, but my only other option would have been Naz, and the last time I'd seen him, he was so doped up that I thought he was dead.

It was a dark and gloomy night. A full moon sat in the sky overlooking us as we jogged down the alley, preparing to buss a move that would potentially generate a $1-million plus in cash. I was already spending the money in my head. I would make sure that all of my mother's bills were paid up for the year, as well as Janet's and Shawn's. Then I would cop Shawn a whip so she could get back and forth. I thought it was bogus how Naz had her riding the bus all over town with their little child on her hip. Philly was full of drug addicts and low-life men that could potentially take advantage of her vulnerable situation. Had that happened, I don't know what I would have done to my cousin. I hated the fact that he was so inconsiderate and self-centered. Men needed to be men.

"Wait up, Jayden. Damn, you know I don't run nowhere. I feel like I'm out of shape." She huffed, breathing heavily already and we'd only run down the first alley with one more to go.

I looked over my shoulder and laughed under my mask. "You better try and keep up. Time is money, and we gotta make this shit happen," I said, slowing down just a tad bit.

We came out of one alley and made our way into the next one, passing two bums that were looking, sitting outside of an abandoned garage.

Jazz looked them over and shielded her face as if they could see who she was. She waited until we got out of earshot and ran faster to come alongside me. "Baby, do you think them seeing us run past with masks on is going to be a problem?"

I shook my head. "Nah, them old dudes minding their business. They ain't thinking about us." I said now feeling my lungs getting tight. I had to slow down a little more and walk the rest of the way. I felt myself beginning to sweat, and I wasn't on that. Wearing a mask was already uncomfortable enough.

"Well, I hope not. That would be devastating." She ran up ahead of me and I watched her cheeks bounce in her tight, black Fendi's. I don't know why I always had sex on my brain, but I just did. Jazz had a cold as body, and even under the circumstances it was hard for me to ignore that fact.

We made it to Buns' baby mother's crib two minutes later. I hopped over the metal fence first, and then helped Jazz to do the same. Once we were in the yard, I ducked and looked over my shoulder to make sure that she did the same thing, then we crept alongside the house until we made it to the front, and quietly went up the steps.

Jazz came alongside me once again. "I know for a fact that that window right there is always open. The latch is broken, and when I was over here a few days ago I checked it, and it still was." She said, walking over to it and putting her gloved fingers underneath the bottom, slowly pulling it up just enough for her to slip into it. She turned around to look back at me. "I'ma go handle the alarm. You chill right here." With that said, she looked both ways and then slipped into the house's window.

I kneeled further and looked around at the neighborhood. It was three in the morning and the hood was quiet, with only the sounds of cars going by up the street, and a few dogs barking way off in the distance. I pressed myself closer to the house.

Seconds later, I heard the door creak open, then Jazz waved me inside. I crouched and made my way inside behind her, stopped in the vestibule, then took my Forty Glock off of my waist and cocked it back after setting the bag on the floor by the door.

The house was dark and had a strong scent of Cinnamon. I could barely see in front of me until Jazz took out a small flash light that was the size of a writing pen, and pointed it in front of us.

She led me through the front room, past the living room, and into a short hallway where we stopped outside of a door that she pointed at. "He in there," she whispered, then pointed down the hall. "I'ma handle his BM."

I nodded and walked up to the door, placed my hand on the handle and turned it slowly, easing the door inward. I started to get nervous as it began to squeak. I feared that the bodyguard would wake up or hear me breaking into his room. So, as I opened the door, I kept stopping to see if I heard anything, but did not.

Finally, I opened the door far enough so I could get inside. I stepped into the room with my arm extended, gun in hand, blinking, trying to adjust to the room's pitch darkness.

Suddenly, I was yanked by the wrist, pulled forward, and I felt something crash into my face hard. So hard that it caused me to become dizzy before I was picked up in the air and slammed onto my back. *Whoom!* The impact from the floor knocked the wind out of me, and my gun slid under the bed.

The lights came on and I was able to look up and see a three-hundred-and-fifty-pound monster with a bald head. Both of his fists were balled up and his face was in a scowl. He had to be the ugliest man that I had ever seen in my whole entire life. He picked me up by the neck with his huge hands. "Bitch ass nigga, you done broke into the wrong house. Now, I'ma keep you here until the police come. But that's after I kick yo' ass!" He hollered, cocking back and punching me in the jaw.

It felt like I'd been hit by a bus. I fell to the carpet with my face ringing and tried to gather myself, but before I could he was on my ass, running at me full speed like a linebacker on steroids, tackling me to the wall, cracking my ribs and my back.

"Get up, you son of a bitch! Get up right now before I kill you." He spat, with saliva running down his chin.

After he got up, I was laying on my side, writhing in pain. I felt like I'd been rolled over by a Monster truck. My ribs were screaming bloody murder, and I didn't think I could take another hit from him. I turned on to my stomach and slid my hand under the bed, searching for my gun.

Once my hand wrapped around its handle, I pulled it out and flipped onto my back, aiming it up at him. "Punk ass nigga, don't move. Don't you move one muscle." I said slowly, making my way to my feet with my ribs killing me like never before. I was sure he had broken at least two of them, but I wasn't sure.

"Just go. Get out of here and I won't call the cops. Go, man!" He hollered and I was sure that he'd awaken everybody that had been inside of the house. He made his way toward me.

I lowered my eyes. "Bitch, get back. I'm not gon' say it again." I raised the gun and leveled it at his head, ready to pull the trigger. I no longer cared about the noise. This big ass nigga wasn't finna hit me again. I refused to let that happen.

He stopped in his tracks and held his hands in the air. "Awright, man, awright. Please, don't shoot. I'm just doing my job."

"Fuck that. Get on yo' knees, nigga, now. Hurry the fuck up." I ordered, walking toward him now.

He fell to his knees and put his hands in the air, looking into my eyes. Even on his knees he looked like a massive gorilla.

"Clasp your fingers on top of your head. Hurry up," I spat.

Now he was being all submissive and shit. I waited right until he followed my command, then ran to him at full speed, took his head into my hands and kneed him, smashing his face and shattering his nose at the same time. I heard it pop against the bone of my knee before he fell onto his side with his hands over his face and blood oozing between his fingers.

He groaned and mumbled in pain, and I didn't give a fuck about none of that shit. I flipped my gun on safety, turned it around and got to beating him over the head with it, over and over again. I watched his skull open up, and blood spurted out of it. He got to his knees and pushed me away from him, standing up staggering, falling into the wall, before kneeling from dizziness.

I looked him over for a minute, then I smacked him across the face with the pistol, punched him into the ribs as hard as I could, and slapped the pistol against his ugly face again, dropping his ass.

He struggled to get up, so I straddled him and got to beating him like he stole something, over and over, switching hands with the gun, back and forth, again and again, watching his blood pop up into the air and all over my black T shirt. I kept going until I was sure that he was deceased. Afterward, I stood up and stomped him in the chest to see if I could jump start his heart just so I could kill him again. Fuck nigga had whooped my ass and that was hard for me to let go of in that moment.

But finally, I did. After I bodied him, I rolled his big ass under the bed and opened the door of the bedroom. I peeked out of it just as Jazz was coming out of one of the rooms with duct tape in her hand.

"Nigga, what the fuck you do? You got blood all over you," she said, looking me up and down.

I wrapped my arm around my ribs and winced in pain. I took a step forward, moving out of the way, and pointed in the direction of the blood underneath the bed. Her eyes got wide underneath her ski mask, then she looked up at me.

I limped past her. "That bitch ass nigga got what he deserved. Come on. You must've gotten everybody else tied up already?" I curled my upper lip, and looked down the hallway. There was one door wide open and the light was on inside of the room.

She nodded and waved me to follow her. "I caught that bitch drunk and out of her mind. It didn't take me no time to duct tape her hands behind her back. I slapped a piece over her mouth too. Her mother didn't put up a fight either. She in there. I just needed to come and make sure that you were okay. It was way too much noise going on inside of that room."

I followed her down the hall. With every step that I took, it felt like it was a struggle for me to breathe. My ribs felt like I'd been rolled over by a bus. I tried my best to fight through the pain and not pay attention to the stinging in my jaw. That big gorilla had whooped my ass.

Jazz walked through the doorway and into the bedroom with me close behind her. The first thing I saw as I entered was two women, one older, one younger, laying on their sides, mumbling into their duct tape, with their hands taped behind their backs. On the bed was a little male child. His mouth was also taped, along with his hands and ankles. I looked over at Jazz and she shrugged.

"What? I had to handle everybody in the room and make sure that nobody got away." She walked over, leaned down and grabbed a handful of the younger woman's hair, dragging her across the floor while she hollered into her duct tape so loud that I grew worried that somebody could hear her outside of the house. Jazz smacked her across the face loudly, and pulled on her hair roughly. "Bitch, shut yo' ass up. I'm finna take this tape off of your mouth and if you scream I'ma have him kill yo' stupid ass. Dig me?" She hissed into her face. "Nod yo' head if you understand."

She nodded as tears slid down her cheeks, sniffling loudly. Though she nodded, I could still hear the whimpering under the tape. She was also shaking as if she were freezing cold.

Jazz pulled the tape from her mouth, then pushed her backward before placing her Timberland boot on to her chest, holding her to the carpet. "Bitch,

170

you gon' take me to that safe that's behind that mirror in your master bedroom's medicine cabinet. I know it's there, and I know how much is in there. I ain't playing no games with you. You dig me?"

She shook her head slowly. "Why are you doing this? I just buried my husband today. I just put him in the ground. This ain't right and you know it." She sobbed with snot running out of her nose.

Jazz leaned down and yanked her to her feet, placing her .38 against her cheek. "Bitch, I don't give a fuck about what you been through, or who you lost. Take me to this muthafucking money. Let's go!" She pushed her toward the bathroom so hard that she flew into the dresser.

The woman hit her head on the edge of it before falling to her knees. Before she could gather herself, Jazz was on her ass, picking her up and leading her into the bathroom.

I looked onto the floor at the older woman. Her eyes were wide open, and there were tears coming down her cheeks as well. She whimpered under her tape and remained as still as possible. I felt sorry for her. She'd already lost a son, now she was being robbed at gunpoint. Life was most definitely a bitch. The little boy was throwing a tantrum on the bed. He looked to be about five years old. He wiggled all over the bed and screamed into his tape. His little eyes were red and his face was wet with tears.

I walked over and picked him up, then placed him beside his grandmother, even though he was going crazy in my arms. I felt that if I placed him next to her that he would calm down a little bit, and I was right. He rolled under his grandmother, looking up at her before closing his eyes.

I could hear Jazz giving orders inside of the bathroom, then a few minutes later, the younger woman fell out of the bathroom and into the bedroom with her nose bleeding. She crawled on her knees and fell onto her stomach, right by the dresser she'd previously been thrown into. "Uhh, uhh," she groaned, crawling over to her mother-in-law and son.

Jazz came out of the bathroom with a blue Gucci bag filled with cash. She sat it down at the doorway, then went back inside of the bathroom and came back out two minutes later with another bag filled to the top. She kneeled and zipped them closed. "I told you all this shit was gon' be here. I knew this bitch had it all!" She hollered, looking over at the trio with hate in her eyes.

The younger woman hugged up with her son; holding him, kissing him all over his forehead. "Why are you doing this, Jazz? I know it's you under there. Tell me what I've ever done to you." She whimpered, holding her son closer to her chest.

Jazz's eyes got big as paper plates. "Oh, so you do, huh?" She walked over to the younger woman and pointed her pistol at her. "Then I might as well get this shit over with, bitch. I never liked you. In fact, I hate you. You're the reason I could never be happy. He kept on saying he was going to divorce you for me but that never happened. I can be one of his emergency contact persons, but I can't be his wife because you wouldn't sign them papers. Now die, bitch!" She cocked the hammer on her pistol, ready to shoot.

"Wait!" She held her hands over her son's head. "Buns never said nothing to me about signing any papers. He lied to you, just like he did me. The whole time he made it seem as if you were his cousin, until I caught the both of you in our bed, but I never blamed you, Jazz. I never blamed you for the things that he took me through. I knew I was dealing with a dog. It's neither one of our faults. You have the money. It's four hundred and fifty thousand. Take it; heal yourself. I will never speak of this night to no one. Just go, please!" she cried.

"You lying bitch! Buns would never lie to me. It was all your fault. You wouldn't go away. Well, now bitch, you ain't got a choice. You can argue with that nigga when you get on the other side. Tell him to kiss my ass while you at it." She grabbed the little boy out of her arms and flung him to the floor, then pointed her gun at his mother, and pulled the trigger.

Boom. The bullet slammed into the younger woman's chest, knocking her backward. She put her hand over the bullet wound, and it did nothing to stop the blood from spilling over the top of it. *Boom.* Another shot. This one directly between her eyes, knocking brains out of her skull. She fell to the carpet with her eyes wide open, and a big hole in the middle of her forehead.

The grandmother rolled away from the younger woman and screamed into her duct tape before Jazz came over and placed her Timb on her chest.

"Now, listen to me, bitch. This little boy is coming with us. Your job is to reach out to Buns' people and have them send us a million dollars in cash, or we kill him and then you. However, if we get the cash in less than a week from today, that's next Wednesday, then we'll turn him over to you, and all of this will be over. But if you go to the police, I will kill him, and then we're coming for you. Do I make myself clear?" She asked, forcing the barrel of her gun into the woman's left eye.

The older woman nodded, and continued to cry real tears. I snatched the lil' boy and put his lil' whiney ass in a sleeper hold until he passed out, while I admired the gangsta that was inside of Jazz, because you could not tell how she got down just by looking at her. I was fascinated and hella turned on.

"Here. You take lil' homey to the car. He out like a light, and I'll handle ol' girl's body. I'll meet you at the car in like ten minutes." I handed her the little boy and watched as she made her way through the house with him, until she left out of the back door.

I picked up the younger woman's body, threw her onto the bed and rolled her up into a blanket before hoisting her over my right shoulder. Then, I put her back down, and kneeled beside the older woman, taking her tape off of her mouth.

She whimpered, "Please don't hurt me. I'm going to do everything that she said. I promise you. I can't have y'all kill my grandbaby. He's the only portion of Bundy that I have left." She cried with her bottom lip quivering.

I tore the tape away from her hands and feet. "Look, Miss, just get that money together and I'll make sure that you get your grandson back in one piece. This ain't got nothin' to do with you or him. It was personal. So, it's best that you handle what you have to and go on with your life. If you try any funny business, I will track you down, and I will kill you with no remorse. That's my word. Now, clean up this mess and keep your mouth closed. We'll be in touch."

Chapter 14

I felt the heat from the roaring flames. My forehead began to perspire as I lifted the body of Buns' baby mother up and laid her down on the slab, before watching Janet slide her into the fire and close the door of the cremation oven below the funeral home.

"Baby, I don't even wanna know who was in that blanket. I know how it goes in the slums, and it ain't my business. Long as you're okay, it's all that matters to me. So, I'll take it from here." She said wiping the sweat from her brown, and drying her hands on the black apron that she wore to cover her street clothes.

I could smell the woman's flesh frying inside of the oven. It made my stomach turn as I continued to replay the conversation that her and Jazz had before she was murdered. It seemed like it was more of a personal vendetta of Jazz's than a robbery.

The one thing that was for sure, I'd have to keep my eyes on her and try my best to never underestimate her for being a woman. She was a true savage with no remorse, just like myself, for the most part.

I nodded. "Mama, I got ten bands for you when you get home for handling this for me. On top of that, I'ma make sure that the rest of your bills are paid up for all of this year, and the next. I appreciate it. Never forget that." I walked over to her and gave her a hug.

She hugged me back and patted my back. "You ain't gotta do that, baby. I ain't new to this game, and this ain't the first time that I had to handle something like this. You forget that you and Nico are just a like.

All of the things that you are doing, trust me, he's already done them a hundred times over. That's one of the reasons I love you so much. It's because you and him are so much alike, it's as if he's still here in a weird way." She leaned forward and kissed my lips.

I kissed her back, then took a step away. "Awright then, that's what's good. I'll see you when you get home. I'll straighten you then." I could hear Buns' baby mother's skin crackling and popping inside of the fire.

Her burned flesh was heavy in the air. It smelled like bacon mixed with spoiled milk. I had to get up out of there.

Janet rubbed my face. "Baby, are you going to help Nico with that attorney, or are you really feeling like it's a lost cause?" She asked looking all over my face, and my eyes last.

I shrugged. "I'ma see what it do tomorrow and got from there. "I'ma do whatever I can to help the homey get out. You know I can't leave him in there like that. That's my brother." I said making my way toward the back door, where there was a red exit sign illuminated. I felt that if I stayed in front of her she would keep on rubbing all over me, and I would never get out of there.

I had to rush to Jazz's crib so we could buss that money down the middle. I was set to get two hundred and twenty-five thousand dollars. That wasn't chump change so I had to get a move on.

Janet rushed over to me again and kissed my lips. "Okay then, baby, just be safe out there. Know that I love you."

I hugged her and kissed her on the cheek. "I love you too, mama."

* * *

When I walked through the door of Jazz's apartment that she had ducked off on, on the west side of Philly, the first thing I noticed was that she had all of my money stacked up on top of the table that was inside of the kitchen. I walked right past her and directly to the money, glancing to my right to see the little boy on the floor next to her couch, laying on his side. As soon as I got to the table, I picked up a stack of hundreds and thumbed through them. "This me right here?" I asked looking over my shoulder at her.

She smiled. "Yep, all two hundred and twenty-five thousand dollars' worth of it. I would say it's a nice lick, no matter what happens with that lil' boy in the other room." She walked up and placed her hand on my shoulder. "Speaking of that lil' boy, I got a proposition that I want to run by you."

I was already stuffing my bundles of cash into my Marc Jacobs duffle bag. I needed to get it all to my safe so I could do an overall inventory. "Oh yeah? What kind of proposition you got for me?" I asked, not even bothering to look back at her, and that's when I felt the cold steel press to the back of my head.

At the same time, a big ass nigga with a black mask on stepped out of her pantry with a shotgun in his hand.

"I say you put my muthafucking money down, and get on yo' muthafuckin' knees before I blow yo' head off of your shoulders. Now what you think about that?" She asked, yanking the bag of money off of the table and grabbing me by the back of my neck, while the dude stepped forward and placed the shotgun to my chin.

I swallowed and curled my upper lip. "So, this what you on, huh? You that cut throat?" I asked, feeling my heart pound in my chest.

She balled my shirt into her fist and flung me against the wall before the big nigga took over. "It ain't nothing personal, Jayden. I just gotta get it how I live. You know how the game go. I just wanted you to see how I got down, because I felt like you underestimated me from the beginning. Trying to play me over five gees and shit. I knew right then that when I got my chance I was gon' fuck you over. You lucky if I don't kill you tonight."

The dude kicked my legs apart and searched me, taking my Forty-Five off of my waist and putting it onto his.

Jazz finished loading the Marc Jacobs bag, then zipped it up, laughing to herself. "If I was gon' stay in Philly, Jayden, I swear to god I would kill yo' ass, but I'm not, so I'ma give you a pass. This lesson right here is to teach you that women are just as grimy as niggas are in these streets. Never forget that." She walked over to me and kissed me on the cheek, then nodded at the big nigga with the mask. "Linda, knock his ass out."

The next thing I knew, I felt something hard crash against the back of my head, right above the bottom of my skull. I remembered getting weak and then everything went black.

180

* * *

When I woke up, I felt like there was something heavy on my chest. I opened my eyes and tried to focus. The pain in my ribs was so intense that I could barely exhale without feeling like I was going to holler out in pain. I tried to sit up, and that's when the heavy object fell off of me. I looked down to see the little boy. He had two bullet holes in his head, with blood running out of them. His eyes were closed, and there was so much blood all over him and me that I felt as if I was stuck to the floor in it.

I rushed to my feet and staggered upon them, trying to gain my balance while holding my ribs. I looked around the apartment and saw that it was deserted, blood all over the carpet, and the front door was wide open. I fell with my back against the wall, breathing hard, looking down at the little boy and wondering what Jazz's purpose had been for kidnapping him in the first place. We could have easily killed him alongside his mother. None of it made any sense.

I staggered into the kitchen, holding my ribs. I went into the sink, grabbed a wet dish towel and began wiping down anything that I think I could have touched. After I finished with that, I rung the towel out as much as I could before putting it into my pocket, and leaving her apartment.

After I got back to Janet's crib, I jumped into the shower and barely had time to wash all of the blood off of me before she was knocking on the door in a frenzy.

I continued to cleanse myself before acknowledging her. "Who is it?" I asked, wincing in pain. Once again, I grabbed my ribs as I turned the water off and grabbed a towel.

"Baby, it's me. Nico said he needs for us to come to the prison right away so he can holler at you. He said it's very important." She hollered, and tried to open the door but I'd locked the door from fear that Whitney would waltz in and see all of the blood that I was covered in.

I got out and wrapped a towel around me, and stuffed all of the bloody clothes into the hamper before opening the door. "Aiight, just let me get dressed first, and then I'll be down. Did he say what was good?" I asked, walking over to my dresser and opening it up. Then, I took out a pair of clean Polo boxers, dropping my towel and pulling them up while she looked me over with hunger in her eyes.

She shook her head. "All he said was that I needed to get you down there, and that he could be coming home within the next week or so. I don't know what he means by that." She sighed. "But I'll meet you in the car."

As she walked out of the room, Whitney walked into it with a sad look on her face. "I don't think you should go, Jayden."

I frowned and looked her over closely while I slipped into some Gucci shorts and a black beater. I walked to the closet and took out a black and gray Gucci button up, and pulled out a pair of black and gray Jordan Retro 3's. "What's the matter, baby? Why you say that?" I came over and sat on the bed so I could put my shoes on one at a time.

She came further into the room and shook her head. "I just heard them talking, that's all. I think the police have been out to see my brother in regards to Lincoln's murder, and for some reason I think he's trying to pin it on you. I mean, I'm not sure, but my mother had him on speaker phone while she was in the kitchen cooking last night, and he kept on saying that he couldn't sit in that prison for too much longer. That you should be there and not him, and that if you weren't going to get him a better lawyer, then he would have to play the game however he had to." She exhaled loudly. "Did you kill Lincoln, Jayden? Please be honest with me because I don't know what to think right now. I mean, I know my brother had something to do with it. He never liked Lincoln, and I knew that one day something would happen. I just didn't fathom that it would be this severe. I don't know who to trust." She lowered her head and then looked up to me again. "So, did you?"

I stood up and shook my head. "N'all, I ain't have nothin' against Lincoln. I didn't kill him. I had no reason to, and I don't want to speak on if Nico did or not. I think that's between the two of you." I grabbed her shoulders and looked into her eyes. "Do you believe me?"

She nodded. "Yeah, I do. I also believe that Nico did kill him, and that you had something to do with it. Maybe you knocked off his father or something, and if you did, I don't even want to know. The bottom line is that Nico is up to something, so you better be careful. Trust me on this." She hugged me briefly and walked out of the room, leaving me with my own thoughts.

On the one hand, I was seething for how Jazz had got down on me. Stuck me for two hunnit plus bands, made me get rid of a body for her, then left a little kid's body on top of me after her croonie had knocked me out with a gun-butt to the back of the head. I felt betrayed, blindsided, and I knew that one day I would track her down and make her pay.

Then, if that wasn't enough, now I had to determine if my right hand man was working with the law in an attempt to set me up, so I could be the one behind bars and he could go free. I felt like everybody in the word was against me, with the exception of Whitney, but I was used to fighting against all odds and prevailing. I refused to fold and would do none of the sort while under these conditions.

* * *

Nico sat on the edge of his seat and wiped his forehead, looking from one side of the visiting room unto the next. He looked irritated and as if in any minute he was about to blow. I didn't give a fuck because of what he'd just requested of me.

I mugged him with hatred as I felt my ribs throbbing, and the back of my head banging from where I'd been attacked by Jazz's goon. I wanted to get up out of my seat and leave the visiting room, but before I did I had to see where he was coming from.

"So, you mean to tell me that you want me to help you blame their murders on my cousin Naz, get him pinched, and then they'd spring you?" I asked disbelievingly.

He pulled on his nose and sucked his teeth loudly. "Nigga, you done asked me the same shit three times now. You know what the fuck I'm asking you. I heard that nigga done turned into a straight dope feen anyway. He ain't doing nothing out there. We can rollover on him, and be back together, my nigga. I got the info on so many licks that we can hit when I get out. I'm telling you, we'll be rich in a matter of months. Word is bond." He picked up his Cherry Pepsi and took a long swallow from the bottle. "Oh, they gave me bail, too. I used that lawyer that you dropped the fifty gees for to get my PO to drop the hold. Plus, she thinking I'm working with the local authorities to solve a murder, so she with me getting out. Instead of hitting Gerald Boyle with that hunnit bands, I'm a have you drop another fifty so I can get out, and do my thing from there. Once out, the police gon' give me a month to come up with everything that I need to present them with the case. I might just get that nigga Naz fucked up, and trip him into saying that he killed them while I got on a wire or somethin'. That way you might not have to snitch on that nigga at all, nah'mean? Why you looking at me like that?" he asked scrunching his face into a scowl.

I shook my head slowly and was happy that Janet had went to the car already. "Because I never thought I'd see the day when you turned into a bitch ass nigga." Now I was sitting on the edge of my seat. "You talking about snitching like it's the most natural thing in the world, and you expecting me to be on board with this shit? Nigga, before I snitch or pin a case on any nigga, I'd rather a muhfucka put a bullet right here." I said poking my forehead hard.

Nico lowered his eyes and clenched his jaw. "Nigga, you ain't got no muthafucking choice. If you don't get me out of here soon, I'ma get out of this muhfucka on my own, and when I do, I'm putting two in yo' dome, and the rest in your mother's head, bitch nigga. Yeah, how you love that? You see, it's bigger than me and you now. You fucking with my freedom, and since you doing that, anything goes. You know how I get down. I'ma do anything that I gotta do to get out of this bitch! I don't give a fuck about you, that nigga Naz, nobody! Fuck the world. Now pick yo' poison."

I smiled and looked into his sinister eyes, nodding. "Nigga, yo' mama in the car. You sitting yo' dumb ass right here, threatening mine, and yours is in the car. That make sense to you?" I asked, feeling my heart pounding. I felt like I could kill Nico with no remorse. I was that heated.

He laughed out loud. "I grew up with you, Jayden. You really ain't no killa. You're more of a bitch than anything. All that killa shit you did, it was because of who you were rolling with. If it was up to you, we would've left all of our enemies greeting cards instead of lead all up in they ass. Nigga, I ain't worried about you doing shit to my mother, 'cause you's-a bitch! I should've fucked you instead of cuffed yo' soft ass. Have my bail money by the morning or I'ma figure shit out on my own, and you ain't gon' like that. Remember the order. First you, and then your mother. Pow, pow." He said, making his index finger and thumb into a gun before scooting away from the table and walking away, laughing to himself.

I sat there for a long time, hearing his words replay themselves in my head over and over again, until finally I got up and left the prison. I knew without a shadow of a doubt that I was going to have to kill Nico whenever he got out. I just hoped that the law didn't intervene before I had the chance to.

Chapter 15

It had been two weeks since I'd sat in front of Nico, and he'd made his threats on mine and my mother's life. There was no way that I was about to put up fifty gees for an ungrateful ass nigga who thought it was sweet. He kept on saying that he would get out on his own, and that's what I was waiting for. I'd already sat my cousin Naz down and told him what Nico had proposed, and he was ready to get himself arrested just so he could go on the inside and kill Nico in cold blood.

Kilroy caught wind of what Nico had proposed and got so heated that I had to calm him down. He kept on saying, "Nah, son, we don't do that snitch shit. Kid gotta pay for his sins as soon as his feet touch the pavement in Philly. Word is bond, I'm killing that nigga for free." He and Poppa shook up as both of them agreed on Nico's execution.

By the fourth week, after me and Nico's visit, he'd stopped reaching out to everybody in the crib, or so I was led to believe, because every time I asked one of the women if they'd heard from him, they said that they didn't. Janet told me that Nico had cleared everybody off of his visiting list, and the last word she'd heard from him, he'd said that he wanted to be alone so he could get his mind together. I could tell that hearing that crushed her little heart because I'd caught her more than once moping around the house with her head down and shoulders slouched.

Whitney's birthday fell on August 23rd, a Friday, and after taking her out on the town where we'd gone to a five star restaurant by the name of

Saleno's, and riding through down town Philly in a carriage while two white horses led the way, we hit up Rasta's night club where we danced for two hours straight, before heading back to Janet's place.

Before I could get the front door closed, Whitney was all over me— sucking on my neck and trying to rip my shirt off of me. I kicked the door closed and picked her up, allowing her to wrap her thick thighs around my body, while I tongued her down and gripped that fat ass in my hands. Her red Prada skirt was up and around her waist, and she was breathing hard.

"Take me right here, Jayden. I don't care of my mother walks in. Take me right here, right now. I need it." She wiggled out of my embrace, dropped and unbuckled my Ferragamo belt. Then, she unbuttoned my pants, reaching inside and pulling my dick out, licking all over the head. "Umm, daddy, I want this dick so bad tonight, and then we're out of here tomorrow. I can't wait." She said before sucking me into her mouth, and spearing her head into my lap while her tongue licked up and down my pee hole, driving me crazy.

I grabbed a handful of her hair and humped into her mouth with my eyes closed. Her mouth felt so right, and in my opinion there was nothing like getting some good brain from a bad broad, especially if she knew what she was doing, and Whitney most certainly did. In fact, she was handling her business so well that I didn't know how much longer I could hold out. It was feeling that good. "Huh, huh, huh, aww shit, baby, wait. Hold up, ma. Hell n'all, this yo' day. It's supposed to be all about you." I said pushing her head away, causing her to make a loud sucking noise as my penis detached from her mouth.

I pulled here up by her hair, then sucked all over her neck while sliding my hand into her satin panties, rubbing up and down her naked sex lips. She was dripping wet already, and I couldn't wait to hit that pussy.

I picked her up, and she instinctively wrapped her legs around my waist again. "Come on, boo, let me take you upstairs so I can wear this pussy out. You ready for me?"

"Unn, yes, daddy. Please. At least give me a lil' taste down here. I can't make it all the way up the stairs. It's my day, and I want it right now," she demanded, slipping out of my arms again before going to the couch and bending over it, after wiggling her hips and pulling her skirt up at the same time. She looked over her shoulder at me, spreading her legs. "Fuck me right here. I need you, Jayden, now!"

I walked behind her, already stroking my dick, kneeling just a little bit to get into position. I rubbed all over that juicy ass, smacking the cheeks, then pulling them apart so I could see her little crinkle. I leaned down and licked up and down her crease, then placed my dick on her pussy lips and slammed forward while she held them apart for me.

"Uhhh! Jayden, now fuck me, daddy. Fuck me hard, please. I'm the birthday girl." She slammed back into my lap, then fell forward before slamming back again, sucking my pipe into her body, soaking it almost immediately.

I grabbed them hips and got to fucking her as hard as I could while she screamed and yelped at the top of her lungs. Her fat booty crashed into my lower abs, then jiggled with every thrust. Since I'd been fucking her, she looked as if she'd gotten thicker. That ass had gotten fatter and I was loving it.

"It's. My. Birthday, daddy. It's. My. Birthday, daddy. Fuck me, fuck me, harder, harder, unn-a, unn-a, yes, yes, uhh-shit, yes!" she moaned at the top of her lungs, lowering her head to the cushions of the couch.

I straightened my back and got to long-stroking that pussy with my eyes closed. It felt so hot and wet. Her juices were making loud squishing sounds. Our skins slapped into each other over and over again. "It's yo' birthday, baby. It's yo' birthday. Fuck, it's so good." I gripped them hips tighter and sped up the pace, slamming into her, getting lost deep within her womb. "It's yo' birthday, lil' mama."

Chick-chick!

I felt something slam into the back of my head, and then it was pressing hard into my skull. I froze, then tried my best to turn around so I could see what was going on, just as Whitney screamed at the top of her lungs, "Nico, noooo!"

Nico pushed me up off of Whitney, causing me to fall onto the carpet, then the lights flipped on in the front room, allowing me to see him as clear as day, before he stepped over me with a Mossberg pump in his hands. "You bitch ass nigga, you got the nerves to be fucking my baby sister, in my mother's house, after I told you to stay away from her!" He lowered his eyes and placed his finger on the trigger. "Ain't shit finna stop me from kill you nigga, word is bond. Y'all get the fuck out of here, right now. Go upstairs!" He hollered to Whitney and Janet as they looked on with their mouths wide open, though he never took his eyes off of me.

Whitney ran over and fell on top of me with her back to my chest. "You can't kill him, Nico. I'm... I'm pregnant."

To be continued ...

Submission Guidelines:

Submit the first three chapters of your completed manuscript to ldpsubmissions@gmail.com, subject line: Your book's title. The manuscript must be in a .doc file and sent as an attachment. Document should be in Times New Roman, double spaced and in size 12 font. Also, provide your synopsis and full contact information. If sending multiple submissions, they must each be in a separate email.

Have a story but no way to send it electronically? You can still submit to LDP/Ca$h Presents. Send in the first three chapters, written or typed, of your completed manuscript to:

**LDP: Submissions Dept
Po Box 870494
Mesquite, Tx 75187**

DO NOT send original manuscript. Must be a duplicate.

Provide your synopsis and a cover letter containing your full contact information.

Thanks for considering LDP and Ca$h Presents.

Rotten To The Core

Coming Soon from Lock Down Publications/Ca$h Presents

BOW DOWN TO MY GANGSTA

By **Ca$h**

TORN BETWEEN TWO

By **Coffee**

BLOOD STAINS OF A SHOTTA **III**

By **Jamaica**

WHEN THE STREETS CLAP BACK **III**

By **Jibril Williams**

STEADY MOBBIN

By **Marcellus Allen**

BLOOD OF A BOSS **V**

By **Askari**

LOYAL TO THE GAME **IV**

By **T.J. & Jelissa**

A DOPEBOY'S PRAYER **II**

By **Eddie "Wolf" Lee**

IF LOVING YOU IS WRONG… **III**

LOVE ME EVEN WHEN IT HURTS

By **Jelissa**

TRAPHOUSE KING **II**

By **Hood Rich**

BLAST FOR ME **II**

RAISED AS A GOON **V**

By **Ghost**

ADDICTIED TO THE DRAMA **III**

By **Jamila Mathis**

LIPSTICK KILLAH **III**

By **Mimi**

WHAT BAD BITCHES DO **III**

By **Aryanna**

THE COST OF LOYALTY **II**

By **Kweli**

SHE FELL IN LOVE WITH A REAL ONE

By **Tamara Butler**

LOVE SHOULDN'T HURT II

By **Meesha**

CORRUPTED BY A GANGSTA **II**

By **Destiny Skai**

SHE FELL IN LOVE WITH A REAL ONE II

By **Tamara Butler**

A GANGSTER'S CODE II

By **J-Blunt**

TRUE SAVAGE 5

By **Chris Green**

KING OF NEW YORK
By **TJ EDWARDS**
CRIME OF PASSION
By **MiMi**
CUM FOR ME 4
LDP Compilation

Available Now

RESTRAINING ORDER **I & II**
By **CA$H & Coffee**
LOVE KNOWS NO BOUNDARIES **I II &**
III
By **Coffee**
RAISED AS A GOON I, II, III & IV
BRED BY THE SLUMS I, II, III
BLAST FOR ME
By **Ghost**
LAY IT DOWN **I & II**
LAST OF A DYING BREED
BLOOD STAINS OF A SHOTTA I & II
By **Jamaica**
LOYAL TO THE GAME
LOYAL TO THE GAME II
LOYAL TO THE GAME III
By **TJ & Jelissa**
BLOODY COMMAS I, II & III
SKI MASK CARTEL I & II
By **T.J. Edwards**
IF LOVING HIM IS WRONG…I & II
By **Jelissa**
WHEN THE STREETS CLAP BACK I & II
By **Jibril Williams**
A DISTINGUISHED THUG STOLE MY
HEART I II & III

LOVE SHOULDN'T HURT
By **Meesha**
A GANGSTER'S CODE
By **J-Blunt**
PUSH IT TO THE LIMIT
By **Bre' Hayes**
BLOOD OF A BOSS **I, II, III & IV**
By **Askari**
THE STREETS BLEED MURDER **I, II &
III**
THE HEART OF A GANGSTA I II& III
By **Jerry Jackson**
CUM FOR ME
CUM FOR ME 2
CUM FOR ME 3
An LDP Erotica Collaboration
BRIDE OF A HUSTLA **I II & II**
THE FETTI GIRLS **I, II& III**
CORRUPTED BY A GANGSTA
By **Destiny Skai**
WHEN A GOOD GIRL GOES BAD
By **Adrienne**
A GANGSTER'S REVENGE **I II III & IV**
THE BOSS MAN'S DAUGHTERS
THE BOSS MAN'S DAUGHTERS II
THE BOSSMAN'S DAUGHTERS III
THE BOSSMAN'S DAUGHTERS IV
A SAVAGE LOVE **I & II**

BAE BELONGS TO ME
A HUSTLER'S DECEIT I, II
WHAT BAD BITCHES DO I, II
By **Aryanna**
A KINGPIN'S AMBITON
A KINGPIN'S AMBITION **II**
I MURDER FOR THE DOUGH
By **Ambitious**
TRUE SAVAGE
TRUE SAVAGE II
TRUE SAVAGE **III**
TRUE SAVAGE **IV**
By **Chris Green**
A DOPEBOY'S PRAYER
By **Eddie "Wolf" Lee**
THE KING CARTEL **I, II & III**
By **Frank Gresham**
THESE NIGGAS AIN'T LOYAL **I, II & III**
By **Nikki Tee**
GANGSTA SHYT **I II &III**
By **CATO**
THE ULTIMATE BETRAYAL
By **Phoenix**
Boss'n Up I, II & III
By **Royal Nicole**
I LOVE YOU TO DEATH
By **Destiny J**
I RIDE FOR MY HITTA

I STILL RIDE FOR MY HITTA
By **Misty Holt**
LOVE & CHASIN' PAPER
By **Qay Crockett**
TO DIE IN VAIN
By **ASAD**
BROOKLYN HUSTLAZ
By **Boogsy Morina**
BROOKLYN ON LOCK I & II
By **Sonovia**
GANGSTA CITY
By **Teddy Duke**
A DRUG KING AND HIS DIAMOND I & II
A DOPEMAN'S RICHES
By **Nicole Goosby**
TRAPHOUSE KING
By **Hood Rich**
LIPSTICK KILLAH **I, II**
By **Mimi**
A GANGSTER'S CODE
By **J-Blunt**
WHO SHOT YA
By **Renta**
SHE FELL IN LOVE WITH A REAL
By **Tamara Butler**

BOOKS BY LDP'S CEO, CA$H

TRUST IN NO MAN
TRUST IN NO MAN 2
TRUST IN NO MAN 3
BONDED BY BLOOD
SHORTY GOT A THUG
THUGS CRY
THUGS CRY 2
THUGS CRY 3
TRUST NO BITCH
TRUST NO BITCH 2
TRUST NO BITCH 3
TIL MY CASKET DROPS
RESTRAINING ORDER
RESTRAINING ORDER 2
IN LOVE WITH A CONVICT

Coming Soon

BONDED BY BLOOD 2
BOW DOWN TO MY GANGSTA